My life changed in an instant,

ALTERED BY FIRE,

*irreparably damaged.
Just like me.*

*I'm a broken, damaged soul on the run
from a very real sort of darkness.*

Altered

THE FIRST BOOK IN THE

They might save me or burn me to ashes...

By Fire

UNDERCOVER SINNERS TRILOGY

Altered By Fire
Copyright © 2019 C.M. Stunich & Katrina Fischer

ISBN-10: 1691532193 (pbk.)
ISBN-13: 978-1-691532193 (pbk.)

Altered by Fire was originally published under the title "Five Fathers" with the pen name "Kate Morgan".

All rights reserved. No part of this book may be used or reproduced in any manner whatsoever without written permission except in the case of brief quotations embodied in critical articles or reviews.
For information address:
Sarian Royal, 89365 Old Mohawk Road, Springfield, OR 97478

Contact the authors at
www.cmstunich.com
www.tatejamesauthor.com

Cover art © 2018 Amanda Rose Carroll

The characters and events portrayed in this book are fictitious. Any similarity to real persons, living or dead, businesses, or locales is coincidental and is not intended by the authors.

For Kate Morgan, may she rest in peace.

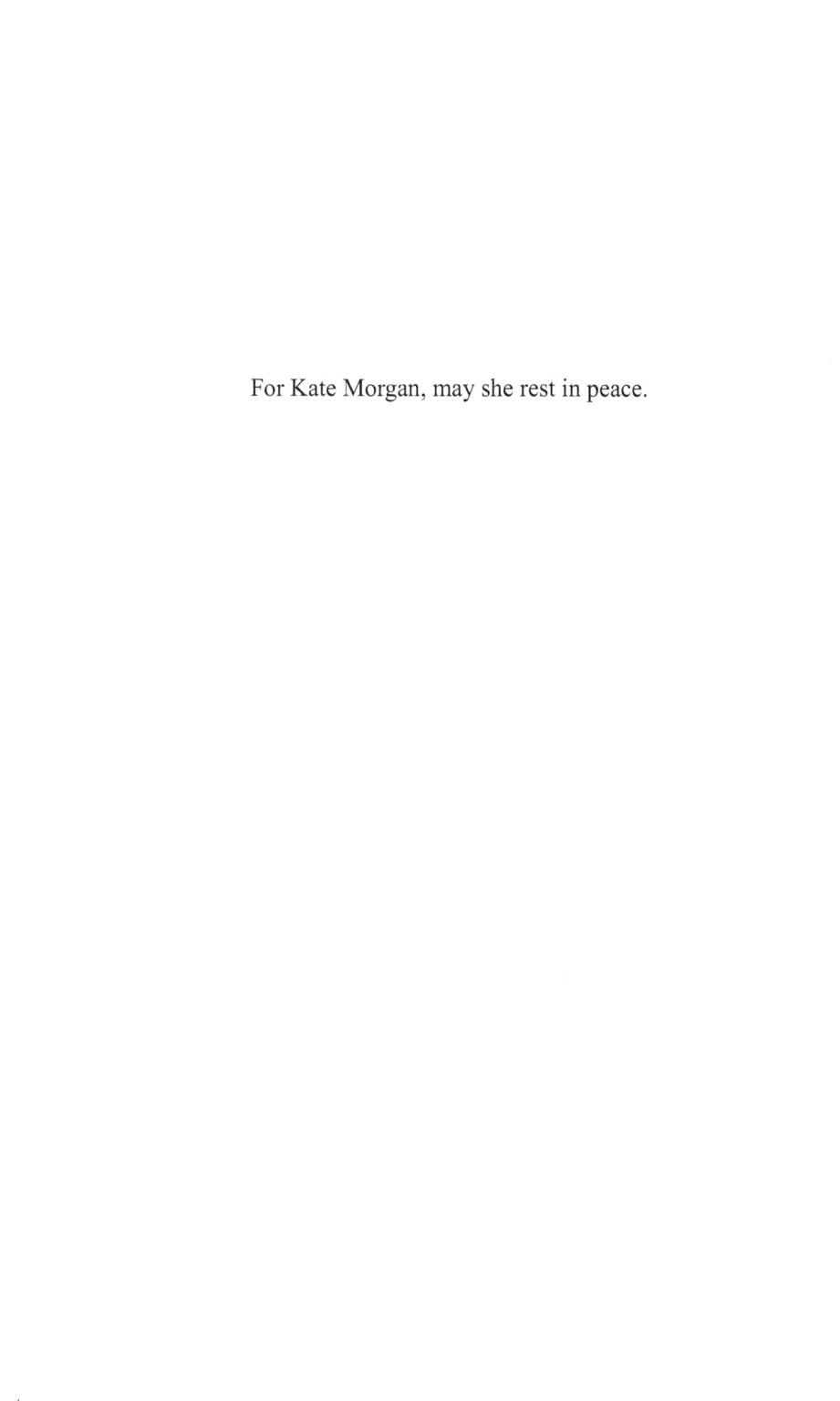

Altered By Fire

UNDERCOVER SINNERS
book one

C.M. STUNICH & TATE JAMES

USA TODAY BESTSELLING AUTHORS

Dear Reader,

Thank you for picking up a copy of *Altered by Fire*. This is a fast-burn, reverse harem, romantic suspense novel that starts off with a bang. Natalia is a spoiled party-girl with serious issues. Over the course of the trilogy, she'll have to learn to overcome her problems if she wants to survive. Expect to see a lot of character growth from her.

This series contains religious imagery used in what may be an offensive way to some (explicit sex in a church for example), and includes power-play and BDSM bedroom scenes. It's a hot, quick burn, and if you're up to it, we welcome you to join the ride.

This novel was originally published under the title *Five Fathers* by Kate Morgan. While it has undergone a new edit, the core story remains the same. Thank you for reading, and if you enjoy it, please consider leaving a review on Amazon.

Love, C.M. and Tate

1

NATALIA

Sin or piety.

Those are the two things I'm choosing between when I stumble up those stone steps, coughing on smoke and choking on tears. As I careen into that church, I'm making an unconscious decision between Heaven or Hell, pain or pleasure. But sometimes, pleasure brings more hurt than pain.

I've learned my lesson the hard way and that's why I'm doing this, giving up everything I know and love for a whole new life. A life dedicated to something, someone, other than myself.

The thing is, sometimes fate has other ideas.

Out of all the churches in town, I pick this one. This building with its vaulted ceilings and stained glass and all its secrets.

This building that houses them.

My five worst sins.

My five most awesome pleasures.

My high heels are loud, almost frantic when I hurry into the hushed quiet of Our Lady of Sorrows, clacking my way across the church's old stone floors as I wobble my way down an aisle of empty pews toward the front of the room, the dais, and the crucifix ... and the broad-shouldered man standing in front of it.

Stopping within arm's length of the priest, my knees give out and I collapse. My bare knees strike the stone floor painfully, but I don't cry out. My focus is glued to the man in front of me like he's my salvation.

But that man, he's going to damn me to hell.

I just don't know it yet.

"Excuse me," I whisper with a quiver in my voice, because my hands are shaking and I'm cold as hell. I fled for my life in an almost indecent red cocktail dress, spattered with blood and ash, smelling like smoke. I'm a stain of sin against the pious, muted colors of the church. "I don't really know what I'm doing here ..." I start, but that's a lie.

Thirty seconds in a holy place and already, I'm breaking the rules.

I wrap my trembling arms around myself and curl my frozen fingers into my sides, waiting for the man to turn around and acknowledge me. As soon as he does, I feel my resolve cracking into pieces, bits of shattered glass that seem to cut.

The man in front of me is tall, taller than me even if I stood in my four-inch designer heels. And he's broad, too, muscular even beneath the black and white robes that cloak his beautiful form. As soon as his gray eyes meet mine, I know I'm in trouble. I don't have good impulse control.

That's why I'm here.

At least ... that's what caused this whole mess in the first place.

I walked out of that cursed den of sinners, that glittering dinner party, with a forced calm born of severe shock. The second those elevator doors closed behind me, I ran for my damn life. Now here I am on my knees, gaping up at a man of the cloth like I'm ten seconds away from tearing all his clothes off.

What is wrong with me?

"If you tell me why you're here," he starts, and I feel my body flood with cold, and then blazing heat. This man is a *priest* and yet his voice is sex incarnate. I can feel it rolling across the bare skin of my arms and legs like a hot tongue. "Then maybe I can help you figure that out."

He crosses his arms over his broad chest, sleeves sliding up a bit to reveal a plethora of tattoos. Are priests allowed to have tattoos? Maybe it's okay if they come in with them so long as they don't get more?

UNDERCOVER SINNERS

I have no idea.

I'm not religious.

I just know that I need a change.

Something drastic.

Something to save me ... and my soul.

More like, some*where* to hide, so that my father doesn't hunt me down and kill me, too.

"I want to become a nun," I blurt, kneeling there in a cherry red cocktail dress with my nipples hard as points, no panties, my skin rippling with goose bumps at the sight of the gorgeous man standing in front of me. My skin is smeared with darkness, and I don't know which spots are blood and which are soot.

But as soon as the words leave my lips, I know I'm dead serious.

If anyone can reform a woman like me, it has to be the church. Right?

I suck in a deep breath as the priest leans down. His warm fingers touch my arms ever so lightly as he encourages me back to my feet, then looks me over. His face this hard, wicked sculpture of masculinity, the lower half lightly stubbled, his dark hair short and well-kempt. He has the look of a leader, a fighter, someone who doesn't take any shit. I think I'm supposed to feel comfortable enough to confide in this man, tell him my sins, let him fill me with the word of God.

Why does it look like he'd rather fill me with something else?

Stop staring at me like that.

I look up at him through my lashes. He's standing one step above me on the dais and it makes his imposing form that much taller, casting a long shadow behind me.

"A nun," he repeats, his low, easy voice making me shiver. "That's a drastic life choice for two in the morning, Miss ..."

"Petrova," I blurt out my real name, because there's no way a guy like this would know who I really am, all the shit I'm wrapped up in. "Natalia Petrova." Oddly enough, his eyes seem to get a bit wider, his mouth tightening. But the only people who should recognize my name are the ones at the party I just left. Hell, I didn't just *leave*: I fled for my life. I can't return to that world. Not now. Not ever.

"You're soaking wet," the man rumbles, letting out a long sigh.

At first, I think he's making a pass at me and my mouth falls open in shock, but fuck. I've been hanging around the wrong people for too long. Of course he's not. No, he's right. I really am soaked to the bone. I didn't even realize it was raining outside. That's how messed up I am right now.

But after what I just witnessed, could anyone really blame me?

The grizzly scenes of my father's actions flash across my memory, and I shudder.

"Come with me and I'll get you a towel and a

change of clothes, something warm to drink."

The man turns and leads the way behind the dais and to a small door. I hesitate for a moment before following after him. The life I've led thus far, it's proved to me that following strange men into back rooms is a bad fucking idea. A really goddamn bad idea. But there are other worshippers here, other priests. And it's a church, right?

"Okay," I whisper, feeling exhausted. Adrenaline and fear got me this far, but those emotions are fading fast, so I follow, ready to collapse. The priest leads me into a small foyer with a set of stairs and several other doors leading off of it.

"I'm Hawke, by the way," he rumbles, glancing over his shoulder as we continue on into a cozy little kitchen. "And this is Colt."

The man in question snaps his green gaze up to mine and takes me in ... appreciatively? I thought priests were supposed to take vows of celibacy.

"This is Natalia *Petrova*," he says with a certain level of emphasis that makes me raise my brows. "And she wants to become a *nun*."

"A nun? With that body?" Colt says, and I feel my lips part in shock.

"Excuse me?" I exclaim as Hawke spears him with this look that clearly says *shut the fuck up, you moron*.

What the hell have I stumbled into? These guys are not normal priests.

"Right. Uh, I mean with a body of sin," Colt

continues, awkwardly backtracking and I feel myself take a small step back. This guy with the bright green eyes and the sandy hair looks even less like a priest than the first one. "All people have bodies full of sin until they enter the confessional," he continues, crossing his muscular arms over his chest. Doesn't sound like he knows shit about his own religion, to be honest.

"My apologies," Hawke says as he puts a kettle on the stove and then moves over to the table to pull out a chair for me. "Colt is brand-new. You'll have to forgive his big mouth. Even with a vow of celibacy, we're still red-blooded men with needs." He smiles at me, and I swear, I feel it deep down in my bones. "It's *resisting* those needs that bring us closer to God, right Colt?" He claps the blond man on the shoulder in a gesture that seems more like a warning than anything else.

"Exactly," Colt grinds out, wincing then standing up from his chair. "If you'll excuse me a moment."

"Send Mace down with something for Natalia to wear, would you?" Hawke calls after the blond guy, and he pauses in the doorway. "She's drenched."

Colt turns slightly and raises an eyebrow at me standing there, shivering, and I cross my arms over my tight nipples which are starting to feel *far* too obvious in the presence of priests.

Suddenly I'm regretting my decision to go braless tonight.

"She looks it," Colt purrs with a wink, then disappears so quick that I don't have a chance to be offended or ... shocked, I guess? Regardless, I'm pretty sure Colt took *drenched* to mean more than just from the rain.

Damn if he isn't right, too. Since when were priests so sinfully sexy?

I groan and rub at my tired eyes, probably smearing mascara and eyeshadow halfway down my face, and not altogether caring. The last thing I need right now is for this fucking delicious man of God to think I'm coming onto him.

Even as my mind is running multiple scenarios of how I'd like *him* to come onto *me*.

Goddamn it Natalia, it's for thoughts like that, that you need to be here.

Great. First, I lie to a priest, then I think all kinds of dirty thoughts about *two* men of God—at the same time—and now I'm taking the Lord's name in vain?

Oh wow, the nuns have their work cut out with me.

"You okay there, Miss Petrova?" This intense, sinfully attractive priest asks me, and I realize he's been holding out a cup of steaming liquid to me while my thoughts wandered.

"Oh." I blush with embarrassment, hoping my devilish thoughts aren't plastered across my face, "Thank you, err ..." I stare down into the cup at the plain black tea. Gross.

"We have milk and sugar if you'd like?" Hawke

offers politely, but his eyes seem to see straight through my soggy red dress as he runs his gaze over me. "You look like you might want it sweet and creamy."

My jaw drops, and I squeak in surprise before a professional smile curves his lips. His lush, kissable lips.

"Your tea, I mean," he clarifies, and I feel my cheeks burn. Of course he meant the tea.

Thank God he cleared that up before I said something stupid like, *no, I like it rough and dirty. Tie me down and spank me Father, for I have sinned.*

It probably would've been hard to play that off as anything else.

Not trusting my voice, I take the mug from him and our fingers brush. Call it a stress-induced delusion, but I swear electricity jumps between us at this light touch. For a moment, our gazes lock, and my breath catches in my throat. I'm frozen, captive, vulnerable, until he looks away and I can breathe again.

Get a fucking grip, Natty. After everything that's happened tonight.

Once again, my mind rattles fractured, damaged memories out for my inspection. Copious glasses of champagne being downed, those few lines of cocaine in the bathroom with the son of my father's sworn enemy … and then …

Sucking in a couple of deep breaths to hold back the tears, I press a hand to my galloping heart and take the seat offered to me by the electrifying priest.

It does nothing to stop the memory of what happened next.

The sound of the gunshot still rings in my ears; the smell of smoke lingers in my nose.

That fire was the last straw. It changed everything. It forever altered my destiny, and my purpose in life. It took a certain type to watch their lover shot in front of them, then doused in gasoline and set on fire. Apparently, I was that type. Lucky me.

"Thanks," I murmur softly, dipping my eyes to my tea as I try to tamp down my traumatic thoughts, try to ignore the horrors I witnessed a mere hour ago, "Father." Remembering where I am, I tack the title onto my thanks, and hope it's the correct form of address for a priest. What do I know? This is my first time inside a church let alone speaking to one of God's chosen.

Hawke pauses as I say this, stopping just behind my chair and looming over me like the Holy Ghost. "Say it again," he tells me, his voice rough.

My shoulders tense. *Shit, I've got it wrong. Will he reject my petition to become a nun if he knows I'm not really religious?*

"Say. It. Again," he commands in a tone that *demands* my obedience.

A visible shiver runs through me, and not from the cold, damp cloth barely covering my form.

From arousal.

"I said," I whisper, licking my lips nervously, "Thank you ... Father."

A sound rumbles from Hawke, like ... *hunger*, and he strokes a finger lightly down my wet, chestnut brown hair. Maybe this is exactly the distraction I need. Nothing could distract me quite as well as a dangerously unattainable flirtation.

Then again, the last unattainable man I'd seduced is now nothing more than a pile of ash on my father's garage floor.

Another bone-deep shudder rolls through me.

"Boss." Another man's voice comes from the doorway Colt left through. Hawke snatches his hand quickly back from my hair and continues over to the little fridge to fetch out the milk for my tea.

"Mace," Hawke replies, and I turn in my seat to see who this *Mace* is.

Dear, sweet baby Jesus. What kind of church have I stumbled into?

I didn't research this; I hadn't Googled the best places to become a nun. Hell, I didn't even know if this was *that* sort of church. I'd run blindly from that party, seeking nothing more than asylum, but *needing* salvation. The church offered those things, didn't they?

But I sure as hell hadn't anticipated this. This, a third man so painfully attractive I was beginning to wonder if this was a test, sent to me from God.

That must be it. I declared my intention to become

His handmaiden, and now *He* is testing me with these men, these angels, these *priests*.

"Did you bring anything down for Natalia to wear? She's been out in the rain and must be freezing." Hawke places a little jug of milk and a pot of sugar in front of me then takes a seat at the table to sip his own tea.

"Natalia, is it?" The new man asks, his dark eyes stripping me naked before him. He is huge, so broad across the shoulders he fills the entire door frame. My eyes widen as my mind automatically considers what it'd feel like to be picked up and thrown over his lap. What those huge hands would feel like on the soft skin of my naked ass.

"Y-yes," I stutter, then realize he, too, wears a collar, "Sorry, I mean, yes Father."

The huge man's eyebrows raise a fraction of an inch before he nods. "Good."

He holds out a garment to me. It's black, and there's a lot of it by the look of things, but it's probably for the best. Sitting here, practically naked and so incredibly turned on ... well, it isn't a good start to my life of chastity now, is it?

"Sorry, I hope you don't mind wearing a nun's habit? It was all I could find aside from our own clothes." Mace gives a tiny shrug as I push back from my chair and stand, taking the robe from him. I avoid touching his fingers, not sure my heart or my pussy can handle another shock like I got from Hawke.

"Thanks," I say slowly, taking the thick fabric in shaking fingers. Would it be too much to ask them for underwear? Yeah, probably. I don't trust myself to say *panties* in front of these men. "I may as well get used to wearing these things. Is there somewhere I could change?"

Mace raises his brows and flicks a questioning look at Hawke. The other priest gives a small shake of his head, and Mace turns his attention back to me.

"Right over here," the huge man says, his voice this deep rumbling sound that vibrates through me as he takes one of my small hands in his huge ones. His palms are warm and dry, his fingers circling my entire wrist as he leads me—in a surprisingly gentle way—over to a cracked door. "There are towels underneath the sink, plenty of them."

I nod as he lets go of my wrist, slipping inside the bathroom and flicking on the light and the fan. After a good, long look in the mirror, I turn the sink on to give myself some privacy. I hardly recognize my own eyes: they're big and wide, the pupils so dilated it looks like my irises are black instead of caramel brown. And my chestnut hair? It's dark with rainwater ... and possibly blood. I don't know. It splattered everywhere; I'm not sure how much actually got on me. The cloying scent of smoke on my skin makes my stomach churn though.

Pulling myself away from the ghostly girl with the too pale skin, I strip my soiled dress off and shove it as violently as I can into the trash, curling my fingers around the wicker rim of the basket. Fat tears roll down my cheeks before I even realizing they're falling, hot salty drops that spatter against the white plastic liner.

What am I doing with my life? What the fuck is wrong with me? A man died *while he was inside of me today. He got shot in the face with his hard cock buried between my thighs.*

Moving over to the toilet, I empty my stomach of alcohol and the lines of coke I did in the bathroom with Kisten. There's no food in there. Hell, I barely eat anymore. I'm too skinny now; I used to be curvy.

Throwing up bile, I stay curled over the john for a long time, so long that my lids get heavy and I almost fall asleep with my head in a fucking toilet bowl. That's the state of my existence now, and that is why fate led me here. I need an overhaul.

A big one.

I must be in there a while because the lock on the bathroom door clicks open and then suddenly Mace is just standing there, staring down at me naked and crying on the floor of a church bathroom.

I'm still in my red spiked heels, but nothing else, wet brown hair dripping over my face.

"I'm a fucking mess," I tell the man who's the size of a goddamn mountain. He's the typical clichéd tall, dark, and handsome type, but hell if I care. I just need someone to talk to right now and he *is* a priest, isn't he?

"Jesus fucking Christ," he says and then pauses, like he realizes what he's just said, making the sign of the cross over his chest and then moving over to kneel down next to me. "Girl, you're in a bit of a shit state," he says, grabbing a washcloth from a silver rack next to the counter. He's so big he doesn't even have to stand up to reach it and soak the rag under the still running faucet. "Err, Natalia, right? Sorry, cursing is a sin I'm having trouble giving up."

He leans forward and captures my chin in his long, strong finger, turning my face toward him. In his dark eyes, I see genuine concern. But like, less priestly and more like ... a man who's seen a woman that he wants to be his.

"Are you new?" I ask him. Surely that explains why he's such a terrible priest? And why there seem to be way more priests living here than one church really needs?

A small smile touches his lips. "Very."

"I'm a mess," I repeat, naked and wet and dressed in heels and blood. Mace's eyes—a dark blue that mimics the sea beneath the moon—take me in slowly, so slowly that I swear I can feel heat sweeping my bare skin, scalding me.

"You're not a mess," he grumbles, wiping my tears from my cheeks and then cleaning off a smear of blood on my neck that I must've missed. "You just look lost."

UNDERCOVER SINNERS

Mace tosses the washcloth onto the counter and leans one of his massive, muscular shoulders against the cabinet door, studying me with eyes that seem impossibly astute, like he can see everything I'm hiding deep down, everything I'm running from.

"Priests give hugs, right?" I ask, and his dark brows go up. He scrubs a hand over the messy stubble on the lower half of his face, eyes glimmering as he watches me uncurl myself from the toilet. I'd rather hug a solid, warm body than a cold piece of porcelain.

"Not to gorgeous naked women," he says and then he must see something on my face because he sighs and reaches out his arms, tugging my naked body onto his lap.

Oh.

Shit.

Maybe this isn't the best idea, after all. Pressed against him as I am, I'm too acutely aware of his strong, hard body.

Leaning my head against Mace's shoulder, I close my eyes again, focusing on his breathing. When he talks, his deep voice—like mountains and shadows all wrapped into one—rumbles through me, vibrating my body and making me shiver with pleasure.

"Where the hell did you come from and what the fuck are we going to do with you?" he asks, but before I can think up an answer to that question, I've fallen asleep on a warm shoulder, smelling of musk and man and laundry soap.

ALTERED BY FIRE

I've never felt so safe ... or so exposed in all my life.

2

NATALIA

I wake up to bars of silver light streaming across the foot of a narrow bed, my hair dry and hanging in tangled ropes, my body draped in a baggy t-shirt that smells like man and soap. Definitely not the nun habit I was given, and definitely not the clothing of a priest, right? Or can they wear t-shirts on their days off?

Wait, do priests even *have* days off?

I have no idea.

I barely know what religion it is that I've stumbled into. After fleeing my father's party, I hadn't paid attention to where I was running. Things had all started looking the same in the wet, dark streets of New York, but when I saw the light streaming from behind the gorgeous stained glass of this church, I didn't second-guess it.

It was a sign, right? From ... God, I guess?

All I know is that I need help. Spiritually as well as physically. Last night my father shot the man fucking me against the wall of the bathroom. His men had held me and forced me to watch as the dragged Kisten's half-dead body into the garage, doused him with gasoline and then lit him on fire.

It was a punishment for me, and a message to them: Kisten's family.

A revolting show of strength and cruelty.

And today I can't even muster enough emotion to feel sad about it.

Kisten wasn't exactly my *boyfriend*. Hell, he was barely even my *lover*. We just liked to get coked up and fuck. My father vehemently disapproved of Kisten's family for 'business' reasons, so I'd been fucking him deliberately to piss Daddy off. I just didn't expect him to be *that* pissed off when he found out.

What the hell is going on?

I never knew my Daddy to take matters into his own hands, but the way he placed the barrel to Kisten's chest and just *fired* ...

A deep shudder runs through me as I remember.

My dark thoughts are interrupted by a polite knock

at the door, and I clutch the sheets to my chest. Why? I have no idea. But suddenly in the light of day, without my familiar crutch of alcohol and blow, I'm shy.

"Yes?" I call out, and hear a shaking in my voice. Like I'm timid, *submissive.*

Screw that.

"Yes?" Clearing my throat, I call again. This time my voice is stronger, and I mentally pat myself on the back. Natalia Petrova is no shrinking violet, thank you very much. The only time I ever play submissive to a man is during sex—and even then, it's only a game.

My father told me time and time again that a good woman is one who is seen and not heard, but I say *fuck that.*

"Natalia?" The deep rumble sounds familiar, and I can't fight the smile when Mace's dark head pokes around the door. "I wondered if you might be hungry? The guys just cooked breakfast if you'd like to join us?"

"Oh." I blink at him, confused for a moment. When is the last time I ate *real* food? I can't even remember. My stomach rumbles loudly and Mace smiles.

"Come on, Arsen is a seriously good cook and you look half-starved, girl," he coaxes me and I'm helpless to refuse. "Besides, you'll end up meeting the crazy fuck sooner or later. May as well be over food."

Gingerly, I push the sheets back from my legs and climb out of the bed. As I stand, I notice the bed is made of wrought iron and has bars at the head and foot that are just *screaming* to be used for something significantly less ... *pious*.

"Everything okay, Natalia?" The huge man—*priest*—asks me and I gasp. Shit. I didn't say that aloud, did I?

Casting a surreptitious look at him from under my lashes, I don't see any shock or dismay on his face, so it must have been in my head.

"Yup." I nod, feeling more confident even as I know a light blush is staining my cheeks. "Who do I have to thank for the T-shirt?"

Glancing down at the soft fabric, I notice with curiosity that it's a *Metallica* concert shirt, so surely not one of the priests? Maybe it's from their lost and found or something?

"Huh?" he replies as he leads the way out of the room. "Oh, that's one of Colt's. He thought it'd be more comfortable to sleep in than those scratchy as fuck nun's robes." He pauses, turning to face me with an odd twist to his lips. "Sorry, the cursing is a hard habit to break."

"Doesn't bother me," I grin, quietly both confused as all fuck and seriously turned on by these priests who seem to break every rule in the book. And I do mean *The Book*.

"So, you guys are all like ... new? To being, um, priests?" I fumble with this question, still not really knowing *which* flavor of Christianity I've stumbled into. He admitted as much to me last night, but I want to make conversation, and make sure it wasn't a delusion.

The black shirt and pants with the little white collar that Mace wore seemed to indicate Catholicism, but what the fuck do I know? The extent of my religious knowledge comes from books and movies.

"Why do you say that?" Mace asks sharply, and I raise an eyebrow at him. Something tells me there's more to this sexy man of God than the caring protector I've seen thus far.

"Um." I point to the logo across my breasts. "*Metallica* concert shirt? Cursing? Hawke having tats? Kinda seems like you all came to this calling a little later in life?"

Mace stands there, staring at me with an unreadable expression, so I rush to backtrack, hoping I haven't offended him. I *need* their help, so I can't afford to be tossed out like yesterday's trash, but I'm almost positive he told me he was new.

"It's cool if you did. I mean, that's why I'm here, right? I need salvation." My words practically trip over one another, and I *swear* when I say this, Mace's eyes heat.

"Well, my child," he murmurs, clearing his throat, "you came to the right church for that."

Without *actually* answering me, he turns back around and leads the way down some narrow stairs to the kitchen where Hawke made me tea last night. As we approach, I can hear the sound of several men's voices, and I bite my lip nervously.

Is it sinful of me to be rolling the sound of Mace's voice over in my head, hearing him call me *my child* in that deep and smoky voice of his? I still have no panties on, and I know without checking that my pussy is damp.

Is it a sin to sit in a kitchen, eating breakfast with a group of priests, while I fantasize about how I might like to corrupt *them*?

Yes, Natalia. Yes, it is.

But will that stop me?

Not a chance in hell.

I guess I'm about to get educated, right?

In that moment, if I'd known the type of education I was going to get would involve leather paddles and crucifixes, handcuffs, and five hard cocks, I ... well, I definitely wouldn't have run away. No, I'd have done exactly what I did anyway and gone down those stairs after Mace.

I take a deep breath before I realize I'm not exactly wearing pants ... or panties for that matter. Tugging the shirt down low, I figure it's a few inches longer than the dress I was wearing anyway, so as long as I'm careful not to bend down, everything should be fine, right?

At least, I think that until ... well. Until I see *him*.

Arsen.

His name implies a burn that's hot and fierce, an

illicit fire set with cruel intentions. I just didn't know it was going to be so literal. As soon as I see his back, I know I'm in trouble. He's shirtless and scarred, covered in tattoos. Big, beautiful demon wings trace down his spine, black as sin, not at all something a priest should have decorating his skin.

My breath catches in my throat as Mace pauses and looks down at me, noticing my starstruck expression with a sigh.

"That's Arsen," he says, but I already figured that out. He said Arsen was cooking breakfast. Well, there's a beautifully flawed man flipping pancakes right there in front of me. I find it suddenly hard to breathe when he turns and flicks a glance over his shoulder, his eyes the color of a cloudless sky, his too-long hair as blond as the sun.

"Who is this?" he asks, his voice like an adder, coiled and dangerous, ready to strike. Without meaning to, I find myself drawn toward him, resting my fingertips against the surface of the table.

"Natalia Petrova," I say, my voice husky and low.

Arsen pauses in his cooking as Hawke looks up from the paper he's reading and studies me. I can feel his gaze as surely as I can feel Mace's from behind me.

"Natalia ... Petrova," Arsen repeats, turning around all the way and handing the spatula to Hawke.

"Arsen," the other man warns, but he's already walking around the table to stand in front of me, his black pants hung low on his hips, almost like they were underlining his chiselled, ink covered adonis belt. He barely seems to notice that my eyes are glued to the tattoos on his chest. "Leave her alone."

"Natalia Petrova, huh?" Arsen looks down at me with those ice-blue eyes, as cold as the frost they imitate, his blond hair falling in his face. He doesn't look like a priest at all, and the way he's staring at me now? I feel like I should run. I don't feel like there's any sanctuary to be had here. "I like the name. Sounds fucking familiar to me, but I can't quite place it."

I swallow hard and take a step back.

Arsen follows.

"I need to use the restroom," I blurt, feeling my cunt throb and the hair on the back of my neck stand up straight. I turn and flee the kitchen, slamming the bathroom door closed behind me. My chest is rising and falling like I've run a marathon. "Who the hell is *that*?" I whisper as I step away from the door. Just as I'm about to turn and flick the lock, the door flies open and I stumble back into the wall.

"Arsen, goddamn it!" a voice roars from outside the door, but it's already been sealed shut and locked. I can hear massive fists pounding against the wood. But this is no shitty hollow core door from Home Depot: this is an original, made of thick, solid wood.

"What are you doing?" I ask as the man stalks toward me and pauses, leaning down to look into my face. He even touches two fingers to my chin, and I jerk my head away, drawing a cruel laugh from his throat.

"Don't you lay a fucking finger on her!" It's Hawke that's shouting outside the door, but it *sounds* like Mace is trying to break the damn thing down.

"Why would you lay a finger on me?" I ask, feeling around behind me and grabbing the very tip of the toilet plunger. It has a wooden handle and although I might not get far with it as a weapon, I can at least make this man hurt if he tries to go for me.

"No reason," Arsen says, eyes sparkling as he steps back and crosses his arms over his bare chest. His muscles ripple with colorful tattoos, depicting scenes from the Bible, most of them the fire and brimstone type.

I'm so fucking confused right now.

"So, tell me, Natalia Petrova, do you like one-night stands?"

"What are you talking about? Why would you ask me that?" I ask, brow scrunched, breath coming in panting bursts. I can feel my nipples pebbling under my borrowed t-shirt, my thighs clenching tight. There's something wild and male about this man, the way he smells, the way he looks, the way *he* is looking at *me*.

I want him.

I want him in the worst, most primal way possible.

Told you I was damaged.

"Do. You. Like. One-night stands? Casual sex?

Quick fucks over the sink in a random bathroom?" he repeats, just standing there while his friends try to tear the door off its hinges. What the hell do they think he's going to do to me?

"I do, yes." My tongue darts out to wet my lips, and I flick a quick look at the sink.

"Good," he says, and then he's stepping forward and slamming a palm against the wall on either side of my head. "What would you say if I told you I was feeling sinful today?"

"You're not a priest," I blurt and Arsen laughs, standing up and throwing his head back. "None of you are."

"Now, what makes you say that?" he asks, dropping his chin back down so he can stare at me with those terrifyingly beautiful blue eyes of his. His blond hair falls across his face, the ends kissing his high cheekbones. "Maybe I'm just having a little trouble controlling myself right now? Do you want to fuck me, Natalia Petrova?" he continues, completely and utterly blatant about it. I hate him almost instantly, at the same time I'm attracted to him. "Because I can make that happen real quick for both of us."

One hand leaves the wall, sliding across those granite abs and flicking open the button on his pants. He's hard. So damn hard. It takes more effort than I care to admit, just to tear my eyes from the straining fabric of his crotch.

"Is that why your friends are screaming? They

think you're going to try and rape me?" I demand, but Arsen just laughs, this cruel, awful sound that I shouldn't like but that I do anyway.

"Rape you? No. They think I'm going to *kill* you, Natalia Petrova." He grins at me, but there's nothing pleasant about the expression. The sound of a gun going off outside the door makes me jump and Arsen shakes his head like he's disappointed as hell over something. "Stupid ass idiots, Weston and Colt. You can't shoot a lock off, motherfuckers!" he shouts, grumbling something under his breath about them knowing better.

I'm downright terrified in that moment ... that, and turned the fuck on. I must be a crazy person.

"Who's Weston?" I ask breathlessly, grasping the most normal part of what he just said like a life raft. I know Colt was the blond-haired, green-eyed devil I met last night, but I have no idea who Weston could be. A *fifth* fake-priest?

Arsen grins at me, and it's the sort of grin I imagine demons wear as they tempt you into signing over your soul. Full of sex, and hunger.

"I tell you they're worried I'll *kill* you, and all you want to know is 'who's Weston'?" His grin spreads wider until he's just *almost* laughing. "Oh, Natalia Petrova, I am going to have some *fun* with you. Before I kill you, that is."

The way he says *fun* makes it sounds like a dirty word. I fucking love it.

I choose to ignore the comment about killing me, because he's clearly trying to scare me.

"Now, angel. I asked you a question, and I expect an answer. " His voice cracks with authority that makes me shiver with arousal.

Jesus fucking Christ. I really am messed up.

"Do I want to fuck you?" I repeat and my eyes dart from Arsen to the door, and then back again. I'm scared, yeah. Freaking terrified. But do I want to leave? "Yes, I do," I breathe out, so quiet I can barely hear myself. He hears me though, and his tongue runs over his lower lip as he appraises me standing there in nothing but a T-shirt.

He leans his broad, tattooed back on the door, folding his massive arms over his chest and not making a single move to hide the *enormous* bulge in his pants.

"Take the shirt off," he commands and my hands automatically respond to that tone, grasping at the hem of my top before I pause.

"Wait. You didn't answer me before," I remind him, my teeth worrying at my lower lip. "*Are* you a priest? Like ... a real one? Because you sure as shit don't seem like any priest I've ever met."

Arsen clicks his tongue, and narrows his eyes in a way that inspires a little more fear through my sex-addled body.

"Does it matter?" he challenges me, and I suck in a sharp breath. "Aren't you already *soaking* at the thought of fucking a priest?"

Slowly, almost without my permission, my head nods in agreement.

Damn, I really am going to hell for this.

"Well, then. I gave you a commandment, and I expect to see my *Will Be Done*."

Oh sweet Mary, mother of God ... I'm so screwed.

Even with my limited knowledge of anything religious, I recognize the reference to the Lord's Prayer. It's not like I've *never* stepped foot in a church before. Hell, my Daddy sent me to a Catholic girls' school for a few years—before I was expelled—so I have a *vague* recollection of some bits and pieces of the Bible.

My hands inch the fabric of Colt's *Metallica* shirt up higher, powerless to refuse Arsen's order, while he watches me like he wants to eat me for lunch.

"Arsen!" Hawke's voice cracks through the door like a whip and I startle, dropping my shirt. "Open this door immediately. That's an order."

My eyes wide, I meet Arsen's smoldering gaze, and he sighs.

"To be continued, angel." He winks at me lasciviously then unlocks the heavy wooden door and throws it open. "Hawke, so sorry. I didn't realize you needed the bathroom. Natalia and I were just ... having a chat."

His wicked grin says he doesn't give a shit how weak that lie is, and my pussy clenches again in arousal. Fucking unhinged assholes are my weakness.

"Natalia, are you okay?" Hawke demands, pushing past Arsen's sexy tattooed body and taking my chin in his fingers.

"Yeah, fine," I croak as he turns my face side to side like he's checking for ... what? Bruises?

Hawke peers at me with a deep frown on his beautiful face before nodding sharply.

"Very well. Mace, take Natalia back to the kitchen for breakfast. I need a word with Arsen." His tone brooks no arguments, and I feel my eyes widen even further.

Shit, is that even possible?

How the hell have I managed to end up here, in a church with five—*five!*—men who I'm at least eighty percent sure are *not* real priests? The fifth man of cloth standing beside Colt, lazily spinning a heavy looking handgun on his finger, has to be Weston.

He's just as delicious as the other four ... how is that even humanly possible?

Tall and broad-shouldered, his almond shaped eyes hint at an Asian heritage, while his bronze tan suggests something more exotic. His coffee-brown gaze is heavy on me, and my insides seem to liquefy.

"Come on," Mace says in his deep, quiet voice as he takes my elbow in one of his massive hands and leads me past the other four "priests" and back to the kitchen.

"Mace ..." I start to say, but he shakes his head,

holding out a chair for me to sit in at the table.

"Pancakes?" he offers, removing the smoking pan from the stovetop and dumping it in the sink. "That fucking unstable dick cooked quite a few before he, uh ..." he trails off with a small, apologetic shrug, and places a huge stack of pancakes down on the table.

"They might be a bit cold now, but—" Mace starts to say, sitting opposite me, but is cut off by loud yelling in the hallway.

"Oh, don't be so dramatic, Hawke!" Arsen yells, and Hawke replies something too quiet for me to make out. There's a pause, and then Arsen, I assume, barks a laugh.

"She's not as dumb as you think, Boss. I'm pretty sure she's figured out the whole *fake-priest* thing by now." He's making no attempt to keep his voice down, so I make no attempt to pretend I can't hear him and arch a brow at Mace.

"Ah," he hedges, "you should eat some of those. You're too thin."

"So you're not priests?" I ask aloud, "I thought maybe you were just, I don't know, bad priests?" Chills trace down my spine as Mace turns a dark, heady gaze on me. The look he casts my way is almost ... pitying? That's not good, right?

Arsen storms into the room, a fury of ink and muscles and male smugness that makes my stomach clench tight. Oh God. He yanks a chair out from the table, spins it around, and flops into it. Crossing his arms on the back, he leans his chin against it and stares at me.

"You are so fucking lucky you stumbled into this mess."

"This mess?" I ask as Arsen reaches out and takes the plate of pancakes, slapping several on my plate and then tossing it onto the table in front of me. The plate shivers for a moment before settling, and I raise an eyebrow.

"Leave her alone," Hawke says, moving into the room ... dressed in Kevlar? Why is he wearing Kevlar and black cargo pants and ... and so many guns? So, so, so many fucking guns. Holy shit. "It's not too late, Arsen, so keep your goddamn mouth shut."

"We're not priests at all and you know it, I know it, but the problem is, nobody else can know it." Arsen ignores what's clearly an order, continuing to stare at me as he speaks. Hawke pauses next to him and leans down, nostrils flaring.

"I will knock you out if necessary," he growls, but the golden-haired psycho in front of him just twitches his lips into a crazy smile as his gaze slides off me and meets Hawke's.

"I could kill you if I wanted," Arsen tells him with a casual air which totally freaks me the fuck out because, like, who says something like that to their friend? "It's only out of respect that I don't."

"Let the girl make her own choice," Hawke snarls, standing back up and staring at me across the suddenly heated space. There's so much testosterone and violence in the room that I feel like I'm choking on it. "I can take her to the nunnery right now. It's *not too late*."

"*Get ye to a nunnery*," Colt quotes, coming into the room dressed in his priest robes and chuckling under his breaths. "That's from a Shakespeare play except, like, it doesn't mean nunnery. It means brothel. Like, he's literally telling the chick to go to a whorehouse. Messed up, right?"

"Shut the fuck up!" Hawke roars and everyone goes quiet.

Wow.

Guess we know who the leader is here.

The fifth man, Weston, walks into the room, also dressed in some sort of religious uniform. Now that he's out of the dim corridor, I can see his hair is streaked with a brilliant emerald green color. He's got piercings on either side of his lip and in his eyebrow, and he doesn't look a goddamn thing like a man of the cloth.

"Bro, take your piercings out," Colt whispers, tapping the side of his mouth.

I'm so confused at that point that all I can do is sit there and gawp.

"Natalia. Do you want me to take you to the nunnery?" Hawke repeats, and I slowly, carefully, tear my eyes from him to look over at leader of the group. I sense an *or* lying in wait there, so I sit still and watch him, the scent of pancakes wafting around me. "Or do you want ... something else?"

"Something *else*?" I choke out as Arsen grins, like a shark. "What do you mean, something *else*?"

"We know who you are," Arsen whispers, almost hisses. "We know who your father is and all the naughty things your family is responsible for."

In an instant, I'm up and backing away from five monstrous men with muscles that are too big, and tattoos, and angry facial expressions. Good God, and I'm standing here in a t-shirt with no underwear.

"How?" I whisper, horrified, and Arsen smiles that shark smile again.

"We're hunting him, that's how, and then here you are, falling, almost literally, into our laps."

"Arsen," Hawke warns, moving around him to take a few steps closer to me. Colt and Weston exchange glances as Mace sighs and leans his ass against the counter, crossing his arms over his chest. "Listen, Natalia," he starts as I look for a way out.

Just a few feet away from me is a back door. There are a few boxes stacked in front of it, like it hasn't been used for a while. Without waiting to hear what Hawke's going to say, I lunge for it, turning the deadbolt and the handle at the same time.

The door opens inward, pushing the boxes out of the way, and I stumble forward, hitting the screen at about the same time Hawke wraps an arm around my waist and yanks me back, my shirt rising up and flashing ... *everything*.

To an old lady standing outside on the lawn in a big, floppy white hat.

"Mrs. Carroll," Hawke says, setting me down suddenly and grabbing the hem of my shirt. He jerks it back into place and covers up all my lady bits.

"Father Dell used to ... set a box outside this door to collect donations for the homeless," the woman says, staring, not at the giant man in the body armor and guns, but at me. Me!

I try to move, but Hawke tightens his grip, the muscles in his arm bulging and tensing like steel. I can hardly even breathe. But having that big, solid form behind me is exhilarating. Hawke smells like leather and musk and *man*.

"Yes, well, that's an excellent idea," he grumbles as I stand there like the typical mob-daughter that I am. Here is a person, unconnected to all of this shit, and I'm not screaming or calling out for help. Because back home, all that would do is get the old woman killed.

That's what my father would've done, and what if these men are worse?

"We'll look into that," he continues, reaching past me with a big hand, and slamming the door closed in the old woman's face.

"Your cover is fucked," I breathe, but Hawke just grunts and lets go of me, before putting his hands on my shoulders and spinning me around to face him. His eyes bore into mine as I swallow past the lump in my throat. I look up, up, up at him and wonder if this is the moment where it all ends. "So, are you going to kill me now?"

Strangely, this idea doesn't fill me with the fear it once would have. Maybe because I know death here, by a bullet in the brain, will be far more merciful than anything my father would do to me now.

"Kill you?" Hawke asks with a long exhale. "Not exactly."

He steps back and gives me a look, propping his hands on his hips.

"Not ... exactly?" I choke out as our gazes meet and a hot thrill takes over my body.

"You have two choices, Natalia: let us take you to the nunnery or stay here."

"And if you do go to the nunnery," Arsen says, grinning maniacally, "you best be careful. We have agents there, too. And they'll be watching."

"Agents?" I echo as Hawke looks me straight in the face.

"If you stay here, you also have two choices," Hawke continues. "Wait us out until we finish what we came here to do or let me teach you."

"Teach me?" I ask as Hawke sucks in a breath.

"Dude, are you serious?" Colt exclaims, storming over to us and looking between me and Hawke like he's crazy. "Just let her go, man! She doesn't need to get dragged into this."

"I can't let her go!' Hawke roars, and my skin erupts in goose bumps. "I can't let her go now."

"She doesn't know anything," Colt says, sounding exasperated. "Let her walk, man."

"She knows enough," Hawke says with a sigh. "And she's Konstantin's daughter. I can't let her go." He stares at me, and I imagine that in a different scenario, hearing those words—*I can't let her go*—would be a breathtaking experience. "I *won't*. Not while she can still threaten our mission."

"So, my choices are go to the nunnery or ... you really are going to kill me?"

"You can stay here until we're finished with our mission. And then we'll let you go. But, if you stay, consider signing on with us. After that life you've led, you'd be a perfect candidate."

"This is ridiculous!" Colt shouts, throwing up his hands and pacing a short, wild rut in the floor. "You can't hire *her*."

"She's perfect," Arsen says, slinking up behind Hawke and taking a seat on the edge of the table. "With all the shit she must know."

"I'm willing to hire you to be a part of my team," Hawke says, "but you'll have to be willing to work."

"Work for what?" I ask, and he gives me a tight smile.

"If you joined our team, your life would change forever. I'll give you a rundown, and if you think you're up for it then we'd love to have you." Hawke arches a brow at me like it's a challenge.

I love a challenge.

"Hear that?" Arsen smirks and throws me a wink. "We'd love to *have you.*"

Blinking at the group of men in front of me, I have a bad, bad feeling about this.

3

HAWKE

I'm probably making a huge mistake with this girl. Colossal.

But there's no way I'm backing down now.

"You think with your dick too often, Hawke," Weston drawls, sitting at the table and tapping his fingers rhythmically against the wood.

"Nah," Arsen sneers, slamming a mug of coffee down, "he thinks with his heart, aww." Arsen taps his palm against his chest, and it takes everything I have inside of me not to lift up my gun and shoot him in the face. The only reason I keep him around is because I figure I either have to kill him or keep an eye on him. He's too crazy to be set free on the world.

"She didn't know enough for us to be concerned," Mace grumbles, running his fingers through his hair. "Not until you idiots started blabbering at her. She just figured we were really shitty priests."

"She's Konstantin's fucking daughter," Arsen scoffs with another scowl. "The second we found out who she was, we should've tied her up and sent him a ransom video. But letting her join the team? Hmm. Yeah, I'm down with that. We can fuck the information out of her before the week is out, everything we need to know about Konstantin and his connections, his habits, the nitty-gritty of his personal life. Easy."

"You aren't going to fuck it out of her," I say with a scowl, and Arsen grins like a shark.

"Really? Because she was about to get naked in the bathroom before you started shouting at me. And did you see the way she was looking at us in the kitchen? That girl was more than willing for any one of us. But I call dibs on first taste."

"You're sick," I growl at him, grabbing my own coffee and chugging a mouthful.

"Really?" Arsen asks with heavy sarcasm, canting his head to one side. "The numerous medical diagnoses I've received gave me no clue."

Sighing, I rub at my forehead. Maybe I should just kill the fucker and be done with it. Sure would make my life a whole hell of a lot easier. Higher-ups wouldn't question me on it either. Hell, I might even get a promotion for it.

"Look, here's what we're going to do. Clearly *I* don't have the authority to recruit for a permanent position within our company, but *she* doesn't know that. For now, let's give her some on the job training and use her as an asset to take her family down. You can all agree that she could be our ace in the hole." I look around at my team for their reactions.

"I'd like to be the ace in *her* hole," Colt snickers and exchanges a high five with Weston.

The two of them look like they always do: playful, mischievous, and curious. They're on my side, for sure. Mace looks concerned, but I know he'll agree in order to keep Natalia safe. The big lug has already taken a shining to her after she cried, naked in his lap. The bigger they are, the harder they fall.

Arsen is my only wild card. Always fucking Arsen. He's been a thorn in my side for too damn long, and it's wearing thin on my patience.

Without really noticing what I'm doing, my thumb strokes over one of the guns strapped to my waist.

"You don't have the balls," Arsen taunts, holding my gaze and correctly interpreting my thoughts. Of course he does. If anyone thinks more about killing people than myself and the rest of the team, it's this psychotic fucker.

"One of these days, Arsen," I promise him in a

deathly quiet voice, "you'll push me far enough."

"But that day ain't today, *padre*." He grins a shit-eating grin that makes me want to plow a fist into his face.

Taking a deep breath to calm myself, I look around at the room. "All in favor of training Natalia?"

Weston coughs a laugh and gives me a sly smirk. "*Training* Natalia? Or training her? Big difference we're talking about here, boss."

Both.

My dick twitches in my pants at the thought of tying that beautiful mess down and having my way with her. She'd make the perfect sexual submissive, with a little encouragement.

"Training her to stay alive and help us take down the most ruthless mob family in this state, Weston," I growl at him, even though my mind is already wandering deep into a daydream of *training* that lush piece of ass.

"Just checking." He shrugs. "I'm in for both types. Colt is too, aren't ya?" He whacks his best friend in the chest, and Colt nods eagerly at me.

"I think that it would be safer to send her to the nunnery," Mace rumbles with a deep scowl setting his features, "but we can't force her to go. So, I vote in favor of keeping her here. Besides, she'd make a terrible nun. Girl likes being naked too much."

I turn my attention back to Arsen, and raise my brows. "Well? For or against? You know this needs to be a unanimous decision."

It really does need to be unanimous; it's the way of our team. We're in deep cover and therefore have no contact whatsoever with our superiors until the job is done. Everything we do has to be agreed upon as a team.

"Hell, you'll hear no complaints from me about keeping her here," Arsen purrs, like he's already picturing Natalia stretched out naked on the church altar. "But I make no promises to keep my dick out of her if she begs for it." He gives me a smug smile. "And she will. Beg. I can guarantee that."

My jaw tightens, but I bite back my anger. Sometimes arguing with Arsen is as effective as arguing with a brick wall.

"Good. We're all in agreement then: she stays and gets *trained*." I really don't intend to put so much emphasis on that word, knowing full well where my team's sexual proclivities lay, but it just slips out.

I'm saved any further dirty innuendos from the boys by the sound of bare feet on stone floor approaching the vestry we're all sitting in. Typically, this room would have been used by the resident priests as an office, or a room to meet with parishioners in. We've converted it into our armory.

A soft knock precedes Natalia before she pokes her head around the door, looking frightened and sad. Not nearly as terrified as she'd been when she turned up in our church last night, soaked through from the rain, splattered with blood that I doubt she even realized was on her, and stinking of smoke.

Something awful must have happened to this beautiful creature to send her fleeing into the night in search of a nunnery ... and that something could possibly be crucial to our case.

But how do we make her trust us?

"Hi, sorry to interrupt," she whispers in a meek-sounding voice, but her eye contact is strong and confident. "I was just trying to make coffee, and I can't figure out the machine?"

A clatter of sound echoes through the badly insulated room as all four of my men, *including* Arsen, push back their chairs and offer to help her.

"Arsen," I snap with steel in my voice, "sit the fuck back down. Colt, you go help Natalia."

"Thanks." She beams at me, like a ray of goddamn sunshine, and as the door swings open further to reveal the rest of her form, my mouth goes dry. Her party dress was crusted with blood, so we told her it'd been thrown out and that she could borrow some robes until new clothes could be purchased.

But I can safely say, I've never seen a saggy black nun's habit look so downright pornographic.

It hangs from her rail-thin frame, exposing one shoulder entirely, as well as the tops of her lush breasts. It must have been too long for her, too, as she's tied the side of it up in a knot, showing off a long expanse of bare leg.

UNDERCOVER SINNERS

It takes me a second to realize she's asking me something.

"Sorry, I missed that," I admit, and hear Weston snicker a laugh at my expense. Bastard.

"I said: would you like me to bring coffee up here for you all as well?" She smiles brightly at me and I swear, my heart stops for a second. *Fuck she's stunning.*

"That'd be lovely, thank you," I accept politely, and sit the hell back down behind the desk before she can see the growing bulge in my pants.

What is it about this chick that stirs my cock in ways no woman has since Portia?

My hand drops to my crotch as I hold eye contact with her. I take my time rearranging my pants, picturing Natalia's slim, pale fingers in place of mine. Unaware of my thoughts, she bobs her head in acknowledgement, and I'm helpless not to stare after her as Colt leads her back to the kitchen.

"If she's to be an asset," Arsen says slowly, in a voice that tells me he's plotting something, "she'll need to trust us implicitly. Every damn one of us. Otherwise, why the hell would she spill the beans on dear old dad? More to the point, why would we trust what she says? Unless she's totally committed to our team, anything she says could be a trap."

"What are you saying, Pyro?" Mace demands, calling Arsen by the nickname he despises even if it is well-deserved. He did a fair stint in juvie as a kid for starting fires.

Arsen gives Mace a somewhat unhinged, piranha-like grin. "I'm saying, we gotta make her fall in love with us all. Everyone knows a woman will do anything for a man she *loves*."

The silence in the room is absolute as Arsen's words sink in. We need to make Natalia fall in love? Then when the job is over, and her family has been decimated ... she gets tossed aside like all our case specific assets always do. That would be a new low, even for us.

"Shit." Weston is the one who eventually breaks the quiet. "We've done some fucked-up shit to get ahead in the past, but making a girl *fall in love*? That's next level."

"Scared you can't do it?" Arsen taunts and Weston bristles.

"Not only *can* I do it, I can do it *faster* than you, crazy dick." Weston pushes back from his chair and jabs a finger in Arsen's face. "Game on, bruh."

The sound of Arsen's laughter follows Weston as he leaves the room, and I rub at my forehead again. I am definitely developing a migraine. After this job, I'm taking a fucking vacation.

"This is going to bite us in the ass, boss," Mace rumbles, frowning in the direction Natalia went.

A heavy sigh gusts out of me, and I eye up Arsen again. "I know. But it's what needs to be done."

"Knew you'd see things my way," Arsen smirks.

"Shall we add a wager on top of it? First guy to get her to spill the beans on Daddy's unsavory business practices gets five-hundred K from the rest of you assholes."

"Don't act like you've already won," Mace grumbles, eyes narrowing. I can see his big hands curling into fists, and I have a feeling that if Arsen gets in his way, he's going to get bulldozed. What a fight that would be. I'd wager five-hundred thousand on Arsen though. Crazy bastard.

Too tired to engage with the unstable fuck any further, I dismiss both him and Mace, so that I can be alone a few moments.

With them gone, I carefully and methodically place the guns we were cleaning back in their lockers and secure them. All the while, I try not to let my mind wander to the opportunity that's been presented itself to us in the form of a lithe, chestnut-haired goddess named Natalia.

Make her fall in love? My conscience knows full well this will end badly, but the adrenaline junkie in me is gagging for the challenge.

Hell yes. This is going to be fun while it lasts.

4

NATALIA

Colt's presence looms behind me, distracting me as I try to work out this fucking coffee machine. I was too embarrassed to admit I'd actually never made my own coffee before, because it looked simple enough. Just put the jug thing under the other thing and press some buttons and pronto! Right?

"Okay, I give up," I announce with a frustrated sigh, spinning to face Colt with the jug clutched tight in my hand. "This thing is broken or something."

The blond-haired, surfer looking "priest" grins at me, seeing right through my shit as he gently detaches the glass pot from my fingers. "Never used one of these machines before, huh?"

"No," I admit grudgingly, folding my arms under my breasts in a sulk. The consequence of that action propping them up to show more cleavage from the gaping neckline, or immediately drawing Colt's eyes is a pure coincidence, I swear to God.

Oops. Probably should stop swearing to God on lies, even inside my own head.

"Sit down and let me make it for you," Colt suggests, and I gratefully accept. I badly, *badly* need some coffee to help with the hangover and come-down I'm experiencing. Not to be dramatic, but this is probably the longest I've gone without alcohol or drugs in years.

Hell, I was even racking up lines on the bathroom sink during *high school*, so yeah. Years.

Just thinking about my borderline addictions is giving me the shakes, and I sit on my hands to hide them from view. Priests or secret agents, either way, I doubt these guys are into the whole party girl scene. Although it'd be hot as hell if they were. My money would be on Weston or Colt for drugs ... probably Hawke for booze. He has that look about him that suggests he has a flask of whiskey stashed nearby.

I call them my *borderline* addictions, because I've seen true addiction plenty of times in my life. I don't have it. I just use the substances as a way to escape my own miserable existence.

"So, do you guys, like, work for the FBI or something?" I ask, tucking loose strands of hair behind one ear and trying not to admire Colt's ass. "And why are you *all* posing as priests? Like, couldn't you just close the doors and say you're renovating?" Even through the voluminous black priest robes, his ass is pretty fucking nice. In fact, his whole body is a treat. The ugly garment he's wearing can't hide the breadth of his shoulders or the smooth, easy way he moves. Like a predator. I've seen men like that before and they were nothing but bad news.

Unfortunately, I'm attracted to the worst of the worst.

That's why I ended up letting a rival mobster fuck me against a bathroom wall.

I close my eyes to block out the images of my terrible judgement and take a deep breath.

"Here." Colt hands me the cup of coffee, his spring green eyes taking me in with a single sweep. "It's pretty shitty coffee, but it'll do the trick." The edge of his mouth quirks up in a cocksure grin. I get the feeling he's a bit of a troublemaker. "Hawke insists that when we're camping a place, we keep costs down. Normally, there's this pricey Australian shit that I—"

"Wow, are you seriously talking the girl's ears off?" Weston asks, running his fingers through emerald green hair, his face still full of the piercings he was supposedly going to take off earlier. "Not every woman wants to see your dick: sometimes they prefer mine. Hell, what am I saying? They *usually* prefer mine."

"Right," I say, trying to hold back a laugh. This kind of stupid behavior isn't supposed to be cute and funny. And yet, I always fall for the wrong guys. Always. "Anyway, thanks for the coffee ..." I trail off because I'm not exactly sure what the hell is going on here. I decide to just ask. There are certain things a girl learns growing up with a father who's the head of the Russian mob, and I strongly suspect they would want to know those things. "Am I allowed to leave? I wasn't totally clear on what you all decided, but kind of got the feeling you're not going to kill me today?"

"Eh," Colt says, exchanging a long look with Weston. "Not exactly."

My brows shoot up. "Not *exactly* going to kill me? That's comforting."

A grin pulls at his lips, and he shakes his head. "I meant, no you can't leave."

"So I'm a prisoner?" I continue, a hell of a lot calmer about this than most people would be. I mean, I'm wearing nothing but robes. I've got no panties, and I'm completely at the mercy of five giant, muscular men with knives and guns who know exactly who my dad is. My chances of getting out of here are not good. So why's my heart pounding with excitement and my stomach knotting with the thrill of it all?

Then again, Hawke distinctly gives off that 'good guy' vibe, so maybe they won't take advantage of my predicament.

And yet the guy you tried to fuck—Arsen—had his colleagues whipped into a frenzy because they thought he might kill you in the bathroom.

"Aaaaaand," Colt starts, making this elaborate gesture with his hands that ends with him pointing a finger at me. "Also not exactly."

"You're sort of ... a guest, whether you like it or not?" Weston muses, slouching in his chair and pushing up his sleeves slightly to reveal both arms covered to the wrist in ink. I have no idea what these guys think of the priesthood, but the way they walk around makes me wonder if they're as clueless about religion as I am. As I watch, he reaches up and removes both lip studs, his eyebrow piercing, and also the silver ring pierced through the center of his nose. As he moves, his priestly robes slide up his arms and reveal more of that beautiful color and strongly corded muscles hiding underneath.

"That's promising," I say with a sigh as Weston notices his bare arms showing and curses under his breath.

"This gig sucks total ass," he grumbles, tugging the sleeves back down. "Pretending to be pimps last year was a hell of a lot more fun."

Both my brows go up at that, but Weston doesn't seem to notice, and Colt is staring at me with his beautiful green eyes glittering.

"All he means is that he preferred cutting lines of coke in the bathroom with half-naked women to dressing up as a sober, celibate man. And also," Colt continues as Weston pulls his robes over his head and flashes a muscular body in a black tank that's so goddamn beautiful I have to look away. "I don't fucking blame him. This disguise is starting to give me tennis elbow from all the jacking off I've had to do. The parishioners of this church are less loose-legged than I'd hoped." His green gaze sparkles with mischief as he looks me over in a way that makes his invitation clear.

I shift in my chair, feeling wet heat collect between my thighs. I've never been good at saying no. Fuck, I've never had to. Any man I want, I can have. Because I'm pretty, because I'm rich, because my dad will fucking kill any man who makes his princess cry ...

"That I can understand," I choke out, flicking my eyes from Colt's face back to Weston's. He tears the tank top over his head and then grabs a long-sleeved black shirt from a duffel bag that's sitting on the floor near the stairs. He drags it over his head, the fabric stretching over taut, lean muscles and ink. The sleeves go all the way to his wrists, effectively hiding all of that gorgeous artwork.

As soon as he's got his robes back on, Weston takes a *hideous* fucking black wig from the same bag and shoves it over his head, tucking away strands of green-streaked hair while he's at it. The shaggy black thing looks ridiculous on his head, like a toupee or something, but shit, maybe that adds authenticity to his look?

"Better?" he asks with a roll of his dark eyes.

They're such a rich brown, they're nearly black.

"Close enough," Colt says skeptically and then the two of them give each other a stupid little high five. "Have fun in mass, West," he says as his friend flips him off and heads out the door into the church.

"Wow, you guys sort of suck at being priests," I murmur, lifting the coffee to my lips and taking a deep, long swig. The caffeine hits the spot, but holy crap, Colt was right: this stuff is total shit. Even though it's against my very nature, I reach over and grab some cream and sugar that's sitting at the edge of the small table. There are cards all over it. Somebody's been playing poker.

"Yeah, you see, it's not our usual thing. Besides, you know we're faking it now, so why keep up pretenses?" Colt whispers, standing up straight and reaching over his shoulder to grab a handful of the fabric. He whips it over his head and tosses it aside, totally and completely shirtless underneath.

Jesus H. Christ.

Wait. Am I allowed to say or think that?

Who gives a fuck?

"What is your usual thing?" I ask, and somehow, my voice comes out husky when I wasn't intending it to.

"Well," Colt says, sauntering over to the table and putting his palms flat on the surface. He doesn't seem to have any tattoos at all from what I can see, but holy hell, he makes up for it with such an intense stare that

I find myself shifting in my seat again, my cunt swollen and throbbing. God. I suck at denying myself anything that I want: coffee, drugs, alcohol, men.

And look where that's gotten you, running for your own life from your father.

Okay, so I don't think he'd ever *really* kill me. No, I'm his precious jewel. But like any shiny bauble, he'd lock me up and never let me go. If he catches up to me now, I'll be a bird living in a gilded cage.

"*Our* usual missions are dark, fucked-up, and dangerous. Not boring as all get-out surveillance crap. But if you meant, what's *my* usual thing ..." Colt trails off at the same time he leans in close to me, palms sliding across the table. When he's close enough to touch my arms, he squats down and pulls his hands back, folding them on the table's surface and propping his chin up. "My usual thing is beautiful girls with their long legs wrapped tight around me. My hard cock sinking into their perfect, wet pussy as they moan my name."

His voice is low and husky, sending goose bumps along my heated flesh. When he rises to his feet, snatches a shirt from Weston's bag and slings it over his shoulder, my eyes follow him like they're glued.

"I'll be upstairs if you need me," Colt says with a shrug of his muscular shoulders and a quick glance back at me. He even *winks.*

If that's not the most blatant booty call I've ever seen in my life ...

I tip back the rest of my coffee and swallow the disgusting grainy mix with a grimace. Even with hazelnut creamer and loads of sugar, it's foul. Next, I stand up and tell myself I am not going anywhere near this Colt guy's bedroom.

And yet my feet make their way over to the stairs and up without my conscious consent. I have poor impulse control; everything I crave, I take. Colt's cocky attitude resonates with me because it reminds me of myself. That, and at this point, I'll do *anything* to forget last night. Sex is good at that, wiping clear old memories. Good sex is even better, and I'm pretty confident Colt knows what he's doing in that department.

At the top of the stairs, I pause. I have no way of knowing which one is Colt's room. Maybe that's a sign that I should scurry my panty-less ass back downstairs and make another horrible coffee.

But I don't.

Moving down the hall, I start testing doors, peeping inside as I look for the sandy-haired secret agent/priest pretender. I only get past three of them before he's stepping out of the next one down and grabbing my wrist. He pulls me into the room and slams the door, pushing my back up against it and penning me in with his big hands.

"I seriously did not expect you to come up here," he whispers, his face close to mine. and I swallow hard. My eyes close, and I breathe in the sweaty, musky male scent hanging in the air. When I flick them open, he's looking right at me.

"Then you don't know me very well," I inform him in a husky, sexy whisper. He grins.

"I don't know you at all—just the way I like it." Colt leans in and presses a hard, hot kiss to my lips, sending ripples of pleasure rolling through my body like a storm. His tongue swirls expertly in my mouth, just the right amount of pressure as it tangles with my own. Before I even realize what he's doing, he's slipping my robes down my shoulders. "God, I hate that coffee," he groans after a moment, and I balk, slapping him in the shoulder like I actually know the guy. He has one of those dangerous personalities that tricks everyone he meets into thinking they know and like him.

"You suck," I murmur, wrapping my arms around his muscular neck and tilting my head back so he can deepen the kiss. He puts his big hands on my hips and turns me, sending us stumbling over to the narrow single bed with my robes all tangled around my waist.

We land with him on top, crushing me into the small, shitty mattress and making me moan like a wanton hussy as his cloth-covered erection rubs against my naked pussy.

"You taste so damn good," he whispers as my fingers fist in his hair. Colt reaches down and unbuttons his jeans, freeing his shaft and rubbing it between my folds. "Shit, condom," he mutters, taking one out of his pocket—seriously bad sign when a guy carries them around in his pockets—sitting up slightly and tearing the package open with a curse.

Groaning, I arch my hips against him and he slips in slightly—just the tip but holy hell, it feels good. Good enough that I'm tempted to tell him to hell with the condom, but fear of pregnancy and STDs stills my mouth.

"Hurry up," I breathe as he pulls away from me, more colorful curses spilling past his lips as he unrolls the condom down the length of his shaft and then repositions himself on top of me.

"You ready for this, babe?" he growls as I buck my hips up and encourage him to thrust me into me. With a groan, Colt pumps his hips and fills me completely, bringing tears to my eyes.

Holy shit. Holy shit, holy shit, holy shit.

He feels so damn good, moving with fast but unhurried motions. It isn't going to take long to get off with this guy; my orgasm is already building like a tsunami.

The door slams open, interrupting our impromptu fuck, and there's Hawke. Dressed in jeans and a t-shirt, covered in guns and knives, he looks like some sort of super-agent porcupine. A scowling, angry super-agent porcupine.

"Get. Off. Her." He grinds the words out through gritted teeth as Colt and I stare at him in stunned surprise. "That's an order."

UNDERCOVER SINNERS

"Come on Boss, this is personal business!" Colt growls, but his leader is already stalking across the floor and grabbing him by the arm, yanking him off and out of me and tossing him aside. Colt slams into the desk in the corner and falls to the floor. Tucking his junk away—including the condom—he rises to his feet and rushes Hawke, tackling him. But the man is *solid muscle* and doesn't budge for shit.

Sitting up, I yank the baggy nun's habit down and watch in horrified fascination as Hawke systemically disables and crushes Colt to the ground, sitting on his back with a single knee.

"You're acting a fucking fool," he tells Colt. "Now say *I'm sorry, sir* and get the fuck out."

"Screw you, *sir*, you're not playing fair," Colt snarls, thrashing around and failing to dislodge his leader. After a while—honestly a *long* while—he gives up and deflates like a kicked puppy. "Ugh, fine! I'm sorry, sir."

"Go," Hawke says, releasing Colt and standing back up. The sandy-haired man gives one last glance over his shoulder, teeth gritted in anger, before stalking out and slamming the door behind him. "You," Hawke growls, moving over to the edge of the bed and looking down at me. "Are you trying to cause trouble here?"

"We're both adults," I declare, hating how husky my voice is, how hot and bothered I am by the display of male aggression in front of me. It's as if they're fighting over me, like I'm some sort of prize to be won. I love it. I fucking love it. "We have every right to fuck."

"Colt is a member of my team and therefore, he belongs to me. He's my property, and he can't do a damn thing without my consent." Hawke's eyes gleam dangerously. "And you're the daughter of the man we've been hired to kill. Therefore, that makes you a part of this mission. And if you're a part of this mission, you're also *mine*."

"Screw you," I whisper, but my nipples are peaked and my tongue is running across my lower lip. I'm way more into this than I should be. Hawke is everything right now. Male dominance at its best.

"Only if you're a good girl," he says with a smirk, kneeling on the edge of the bed between my slightly spread legs. He stares at me like he thinks I'll be as easy to break as Colt. "Is that what you want, Natalia? To *screw* me?"

"What gave you that crazy idea?" I choke out, but really ... the answer is yes. A yes as loud and resounding as the church bells clanging up above our heads. I want him so badly it almost hurts.

Hawke doesn't respond to my rhetorical question, but leans closer, planting a hand beside my head.

"What ..." My question trails off, and I need to swallow and wet my lips before I can continue. "What are you doing, Hawke?"

"Do you do this often, Miss Petrova?" he asks me

in a voice like velvet as his lips brush my ear. Jolts of pleasure shoot through me at that light touch, and I bite my lip hard enough to draw blood.

"Do what? Fuck a fake priest?" I ask, and Hawke chuckles.

"Ask stupid questions." He sits back on his knees, and I whimper at the sudden loss of warmth from his body. Giving me a long, calculating look, Hawke runs his tongue over his bottom lip, and I shiver.

Christ, he's sexy.

Biting my lip again to keep from asking another stupid question, I wait to see what his next move is going to be. I'm praying it'll be to fuck me. Colt got me more than worked up, and if Hawke isn't going to finish the job, then I'll have to do it myself.

"Turn over," he commands me, and my eyes widen. Not with fear. With excitement. Quickly, I do as I'm told, and feel his broad hands grip my waist, lifting me up until I'm on my knees. "Face on the pillow," he corrects when I try to reposition my weight onto my hands. His hand grasps my hair, and shoves my face down onto the pillow where he wants it.

Suddenly, with my cheek pressing into the fabric and my naked rear-end high in the air, I'm struck by how exposed and vulnerable I am. It only serves to heighten my excitement though, not diminish it, and I can't stop myself from wiggling my ass in encouragement.

"Jesus," Hawke mutters, running his rough palms

over the skin of my butt and squeezing. Hard. Hard enough to make me yelp. "You're just begging for it, aren't you Miss Petrova? Just look at how wet you are." His thick fingers trail over my heated core, and I moan into the pillow.

That brief penetration from Colt has me all kinds of worked-up, and I'm not above begging. In the bedroom, at least. I'd never, ever beg in a non-sexual situation; it just isn't how I was raised.

"Please," I gasp out, and one of Hawke's long fingers slips inside me, teasing me.

"Please, what?" he asks, adding a second finger and slowly pumping into my dripping slit.

"Please, Hawke," I groan, desperate to lose myself —and my emotions—in a barrage of sexual pleasure. "Please finish what Colt started. Fuck me. I'm begging you."

"Well, when you ask so nicely ..." His fingers withdraw from me, and I hear the distinctive sound of his belt buckle opening, followed by the crinkle of a condom wrapper.

"Come on," I demand, impatient as ever. I was raised the sort of girl who doesn't like to wait for things, and that sometimes bleeds over into my sex life. Much to my previous lovers' annoyances.

"Natalia, you are not in control here," Hawke informs me in a dangerous sounding voice. All the same, I feel the warmth of his cock press against my cunt, and I sigh with anticipation. "I am the leader of this team, and you are our prisoner for the foreseeable future." He leans forward, wrapping my long hair around his fist in a tight grip and tugging firmly. "Is that perfectly clear, Miss Petrova?"

Practically panting with need, I whimper out my response. "Yes, crystal clear, sir."

"Excellent." He purrs his approval, using his free hand to guide his cock a little further inside my aching core. "Now, Weston is about to begin Sunday Mass, and I want him to hear you scream. Can you do that for me, pet?"

"Uh-huh," I moan, feeling the delicious slide of his cock inside me. He's thicker than Colt, but I'm already so wet it isn't an issue. Once he reaches his limit, his pelvis flush with my ass, he grips my hair tighter and pulls my head back at an angle that's just this side of painful.

Or maybe it's just the other side. The lines are always a bit blurry for me, but either way I fucking love it.

"Good, I want to hear what those lungs are made of," he grunts, then begins to move inside me with hard, dominating strokes, dragging sounds from my throat that could rival any professional porn star.

"Louder," he commands, cracking his free hand down on my ass cheek and this time really making me scream. It hurts. Like, way more than the light spanking I'd had to practically bribe Kisten into giving me in the past. No, Hawke is a man who knows how to hurt someone, so this is a whole different ball game.

A game I look forward to mastering.

"You like that, don't you, pet?" Hawke pants as my cunt clenches his dick in a vice-like grip. "You like that little edge of pain with your pleasure, I can feel it." His hand cracks down again, sending a sharp sting through me, making me tense and then moan with ecstasy as the stinging fades to warmth. His punishing rhythm slows as my muscles tighten around him again, making it hard for him to move.

But like he just told me: I'm not in control. He is.

His hand comes down again, and my scream is loud enough to shake the crucifix above the bed. Or perhaps that's from the rough pounding of Hawke's hips against my ass. Either way, when the pain fades, I'm nothing but a panting, moaning mess, *begging* for more.

"Hawke," I gasp, pushing back onto his cock as his fingers grip a handful of tender flesh tightly. His other fist is still tightly wound in my hair, holding my head up at an angle that just permits me a view of the Virgin Mary statue on the bedside table. "I'm going to come."

My rampant sex life is not coincidental. I'm one of those lucky bitches that finds orgasming easy, even without any clitoral stimulation. Not that I'm ever against the extra attention.

"Make it loud." He growls the command, and I'm all too happy to comply. The fact that he wants Weston to hear us, while he's playing the role of priest ... it's fucking hot as hell.

Prisoner or not, I'm in Heaven.

My screams echo through the little room, but Hawke doesn't release me. Not until he finishes himself some moments later with a roar and several bruisingly hard thrusts so deep inside me I can feel him hit my cervix.

When he does finally release my hair, I collapse onto the mattress in boneless exhaustion. Hawke's withdrawal from my body leaves me feeling chilled, and I roll over to watch as he snaps the used condom off and flicks it into a trash can.

I can't help it; as I watch him handling his still semi-erect dick, I lick my lips.

"Natalia Petrova, you're going to be trouble around here, aren't you?" he growls, watching my mouth with hunger but deliberately tucking his cock back into his pants, then doing them up.

"I sure hope so," I breathe, still lightheaded from that seriously thorough fuck. "Isn't that what all prisoners are supposed to be? Trouble?"

Hawke narrows his eyes at me, but he can't hide his interest. "Prisoners are also supposed to be tied up." He pauses and gives me a pointed look. "I'm heading out," he tells me, as if his Kevlar armor and multiple guns didn't give that away.

Holy shit, he just fucked me while wearing at least three guns, that I can see. I didn't think I could be more turned-on by the whole situation, but he's proving me wrong.

"What am I supposed to do?" I ask, biting my lip. All jokes aside, the reality of the situation is that I *am* their prisoner. A polite one, and not under any particular duress ... yet ... still not free to leave.

He raises an eyebrow at me with his hand on the doorknob. "Relax. Get to know my team. We'll begin your training when I'm back tomorrow." Opening the door, he takes a step out then pauses and turns back to me. "Oh, and steer clear of Arsen. He's a dangerous fuck, and I'd hate to see you get hurt."

"Unless it's by you?" I reply with a sly grin and his eyes narrow.

"Different kind of hurt," he says with a dangerous voice, then turns and leaves without another word.

For a long time, I lie there on Colt's lumpy single mattress, my naked cunt exposed and aching as I stare at the ceiling. The way Hawke gave that warning reminded me of Arsen cornering me in the bathroom. He'd said then that his team was afraid he'd kill me.

I should be afraid. Terrified. So why does it only seem to arouse me?

5
NATALIA

Once the sound of Hawke's footsteps fades away, I find a bathroom to clean myself up a bit before exploring the building. From what I can tell, it's an add-on at the back of the main church. It has sparse, utilitarian bedrooms with single beds in them and crucifixes on the walls, a small kitchen where I tried to make coffee, and that's about it.

Hunting through the fridge for something to eat, I can hear the chorus of voices coming from the main church where, presumably, Weston is holding mass.

Huh. They're really taking this whole priest thing seriously.

Then again, it'd be pretty suspicious if they just cancelled all church services when they moved in. Which begs the question: where are the *real* priests?

Without really noticing what I'm doing, I drift over to a door which I assume might lead outside. Just as my fingers touch the doorknob, a heavy hand closes over my shoulder, and I jump in fright.

"Going somewhere, Natalia?" Mace rumbles, and my breath catches as the sound seems to reverberate through me.

Speechless, I shake my head, hoping my wide eyes convey the idea that I *hadn't* been about to make a run for it. I truly hadn't, I don't think. Prisoner or not, this has to be safer than risking it on my own, or worse … returning home.

"Good." He gives me a small smile that reaches all the way to his eyes, before holding up a bunch of shopping bags clenched in his huge fist. "I grabbed you some clothes from the shop down the street. We figured it probably wasn't safe for you to go home to get your own things, and as good as you *do* look in a nun's habit …"

"It's maybe not the most appropriate attire?" I finish for him, and chuckle. My voice sounds breathy and needy, so I clear my throat to try and get it under control.

Mace shrugs one massive shoulder and hands me

the bags. "Just figured you might be more comfortable. This mission could take a few weeks."

This causes my jaw to drop. "You mean to keep me here for *weeks*? I thought it'd maybe be like a couple of days or whatever. You finish whatever job you're doing, then you move on, and I'm free to go?"

"Weeks, yeah." Mace scratches thoughtfully at his stubbled chin. "If not longer. Of course that depends on the mission."

I peer inside the bags then narrow my eyes at him. "You're not FBI, are you?" Colt and Weston hadn't actually answered me when I'd asked this earlier, and it's pretty obvious, but I want an answer anyway.

Mace stares back at me for a long moment before replying. "No, sweetheart. We're something with considerably less rules. You'd do wise to tread carefully."

A shiver of fear runs through me, but I can't stop myself from asking more questions. Potentially life-threatening questions, but I'm already their prisoner so why not?

"Are you planning on killing my father? Hawke said something about being hired to kill him, but that could have just been like, a metaphor?" My words fall from my mouth like rocks, and I cringe when I hear them aloud. I sound stupid. Like a stupid, sheltered mob princess.

"Would that upset you?" Mace replies quietly, watching me with a gaze so intense it seems like he can see right into my soul. Like he's stripping me bare with just his eyes.

I shudder again, then surprise myself by the honesty in my answer. "No."

My father, I've recently learned, is a cruel, unscrupulous man, and he deserves everything he has coming to him. Of that, I have no doubts. What surprises me is the lack of, well, *any* emotion when Mace speaks of my father's impending death. Because that's clearly what they've come for.

"Will you help us, then?" he continues, raking those intense eyes over my face, but I shake my head firmly.

"No. I won't help. I won't stand in your way, but you don't understand who you're dealing with. If you fail, like so, so many before you have, and then my father learns I helped you ..." A third time, my body shakes with a shudder. "No, I'm sorry, and I wish you luck, but this is suicide."

Mace grunts noncommittally and then looks me over with a small sigh.

"You are skinny as *fuck*," he says, taking note of my tiny waist and thin wrists. More than one man in the past has made the mistake of thinking that means I'm weak. Far from it. There's so much more to conflict than physical strength; that's just one aspect. One aspect I wish I had, but still. "What the hell do you eat? Salad and croutons?"

A laugh bubbles past my lips as I run both hands down my face.

"Salad? I only wish I were that healthy. No, vodka and cocaine for dinner and breakfast. After breakfast, I'm usually passed out through lunch so ..." I shrug again and cross my arms over my breasts, drawing Mace's attention to the full mounds. I'm lucky I have boobs at all, considering the rest of me is skin and bones.

"Are you hungry?" he asks, tilting his head to one side. The man is an utter monster. One of the biggest dudes I've ever seen, and I've been around a few thousand self-proclaimed badasses in my time. This guy, though, I have to remember how gently he held my naked, weeping form in the bathroom. There's something special about this one.

"I suppose ..." I say, trying not to notice the hard spots of Mace's nipples beneath his dark blue t-shirt. He's wearing black slacks and boots now. I guess— like Colt said—there's no point in trying to *pretend* to be priests behind closed doors, right? "But there's nothing to eat here except uncooked pancake mix. And I'll be honest with you: I can't cook for shit, not even instant stuff."

Mace makes this grumbling sound that I'm pretty sure is a laugh, but ... do mountains even laugh? I have no idea.

"Get dressed, and I'll take you out."

My brows perk up at that, and I take a step back, bumping into the refrigerator.

"I don't want to go out," I say, realizing suddenly

how true that is. Even if this place is filled with a bunch of phony priests, my father is out there. And I'm not entirely sure *what* he'll do to me if I step out into the sunshine. Shoot me with a tranquilizer? Kidnap me? Would he let his men gang rape me? I have no idea, but I've seen him do all those things and worse to men ... women ... *and children.* Bile rises in my throat, and I turn away, closing my eyes against the horrific memories.

"You don't have to be afraid when you're with me," Mace says, reaching out a huge hand and using a single finger to turn my face toward him. His smile doesn't reach his eyes, but it's loose and easy to look at.

"Me, on the other hand, you should be *terrified* to be alone with." Arsen is leaning in the doorway, his back to the old wood casing, one boot propped up. As I turn to look at him, he licks the edge of a *knife* and my mouth drops open. His blonde hair is wet and hanging in his face. When our eyes meet, his grin is wicked and sharp and dangerous as hell.

My blood starts to pump, and my throat gets tight, but I'll admit it: I'm intrigued.

"Fuck off, Arsen," Mace snarls, that gentle giant facade falling away as he spins and spears the smaller, but equally deadly looking man with a look that could smelt metal. "Hawke's put me in charge of protecting the girl—and that includes from you."

Arsen just laughs, leaning his head back against the

wood casing and rocking it back and forth as he quietly mouths the words to some song I can't hear. At first, I think this is just more proof that he's completely and utterly insane, but then he yanks out a single earbud I hadn't noticed before and tosses the cord around his neck.

"What's in the bag, Miss Petrova?" he asks, smiling like a shark.

"Clothes," Mace answers gruffly, crossing his arms over a chest as wide as the friggin' kitchen table. He *looks* like he could snap Arsen's neck with little to no effort, but then again, never underestimate crazy people. I've seen many a person make that mistake in the past. My father's right-hand man is clinically batshit. When he found out his wife was watching gay porn behind his back, he put a bullet in her head during *dinner*. We were having *pierogi*—she'd made it—and then all of a sudden, there was just blood everywhere. "Don't you have a job to do?"

"Not particularly," Arsen drawls, giving me a puppy dog look. It's a weird contrast, that expression with his priestly robes, the tattoos around his neck, and the earbuds dangling across his chest. He lifts up an inked hand and wiggles his fingers. "Idle hands are the tools of the devil, and all that. Give me something to do with these fingers, Natalia," he purrs, sliding two of them into his hot, lush mouth.

Shit. Shit, shit, shit.

Pretty sure I've got a problem.

I'm addicted to more than just partying and coke and alcohol: I'm addicted to dangerous assholes. Kisten was proof of that. Why the hell did I ever let myself get involved with him in the first place? Clearly I was trying to piss my father off, to rebel and show him he wasn't the boss of me.

He sure showed me.

"Natalia and I are going out," Mace snarls, moving over to stand in front of Arsen. I imagine that's a movement that forces most men back by sheer presence alone. Doesn't seem to do a damn thing to Arsen. He just lifts his head up to look into Mace's dark blue eyes. "Get out of the way of the bathroom."

"Oh?" Arsen says, quirking a single brow and standing up straight. "Was I stopping Natalia from entering it? I don't recall."

Mace lets out a vicious snarl that would've scared me shitless if it were directed my way. Arsen barely blinks.

"I've always told Hawke you were a liability. He leaves your crazy ass to wander until it's time for shit to go down. You're a nightmare just waiting to happen."

"Have you ever thought I'm *so* ridiculously useful that he has no choice but to put up with me?" Arsen pauses a moment and then in an instant, the knife in his hand is at Mace's throat. "I could've killed you just now and you'd have never seen it coming." He retracts the weapon, grins, and saunters off, spinning the blade as he goes.

"Stay away from him," Mace warns, glancing over his shoulder at me. Whatever he sees on my face must scare the crap out of him because he turns fully and comes to stand in front of me, putting two big hands on my shoulders. "I mean it. His name isn't a joke. If you get too close, you'll fucking burn."

I nod, but inside, I'm already dreaming of the delicious pain in those idle hands …

Told you I have problems.

6

NATALIA

The clothes Mace purchased for me aren't exactly my style: black flats, a long, black dress, and a wool coat. I look like I'm on my way to a funeral, but it's the thought that counts, right?

The guys have a fucking huge black Hummer parked like ten blocks away. I'm forced to walk them in the bright sunshine, looking over my shoulder every ten seconds like I expect my dad or one of his cronies to just leap out at me.

"You really drive one of these stupid things?" I ask when I climb in and look around the vehicle. It's not much of a shocker that the military uses these things; they look like mini-tanks.

"Plenty of room," Mace growls out, his voice so low and deep that goose bumps pebble up across my flesh and it takes three tries for me to swallow. I almost ask *plenty of room for what?* but the expression on the big man's face gives me all the answer I need. His pupils are big and dark, bleeding into the deep blue of his eyes.

Not at all surreptitiously, I glance down at his crotch for proof of his arousal, but I don't see anything and make a small moue of disappointment that causes Mace to grin at me.

"Heavy canvas. Hides all sorts of stains," he says, and I raise both brows. "Like blood," he adds after a moment which is just as sexy as ... well, whatever it was we were both just thinking about.

Clearly though, my reaction to these guys says I'm insane. I shouldn't be checking out dangerous, unpredictable men when what I really need to do is figure out how to start a new life with nobody and nothing.

I should've taken money when I ran.

I'm only now realizing that for the first time in my life ... I'm poor. I've never wanted for anything except love. My dad gave me everything and then some—besides his affection.

We head to a drive-thru, and when I tell Mace what I want, he orders me an extra-large version with a pound of fries, a burger with a triple patty, and a massive chocolate milkshake. I'm not exactly complaining, but I'm full after about ten fries and three bites.

My stomach is shrunk, and I've been through some serious shit in the last few days. Mace raises an eyebrow, but he's a smart man and doesn't say anything. It's only after we've been driving for a bit that I realize we're heading in the opposite direction from the church and out towards the country.

My blood goes cold and gooseflesh prickles across my skin.

"Where are you taking me?" I ask, glancing over at the big man and his handsome face. Why does it look so sinister all of a sudden? And why is my breathing so frantic and wild? Because I don't want to die today, and I have the feeling that if Mace *wanted* to get rid of me right now, he could?

"You'll see," he grumbles, flicking on his turn signal as I press myself into the passenger side door and reach for the handle. If I have to, I'll throw myself out and onto the road. It'll hurt, but it's better than being dragged out to the middle of the country and strangled or shot or—

"A shooting range?" I ask as we turn down a gravel drive and park in a lot filled with trucks and SUVs. "Oh, thank God." My heart thundering, I close my eyes and throw up a prayer. I'm not even sure if I'm doing it right, but whatever. It's the thought that counts, right?

"Why not?" he asks with a loose shrug, a smile hiding in that thick dark stubble on his handsome jaw. "We've needed a woman on our team for years."

UNDERCOVER SINNERS

"And why is that?" I ask coolly. I always expect the worst in people. Old habits and all that. Mace turns the engine off and leans over, his huge, muscular arm diving between my thighs and pulling out a black case from under my seat.

"New perspective on things," he explains as I sit there gaping and wondering why I'm so disappointed that he *didn't* do anything else when he was between my legs. "Better for undercover. Fresh blood in the mix. And maybe then if we find a good, solid new member, Hawke'll finally put that bullet in Arsen's head that he's so long deserved."

Mace opens the driver's side door and climbs out. I follow after, slamming my own door behind me. I'm wearing a bra that's about two sizes too small, my boobs muffining up and over the tops, creating these weird little bulges that are beyond obvious, especially with the sweetheart neckline I'm wearing. Mace, perhaps, doesn't seem to think it looks so weird, based on the way his eyes linger before he tears himself away.

Still, I follow him into the building and take pleasure in the fact that there's a woman working the counter. She's wearing baggy camo pants and gives my small frame a *look*, but it's better than getting that same sort of look from a man.

As soon as I get out there on the range though, I'll show them all how a mobster's daughter can shoot.

Grinning to myself, I watch as Mace pays the fees,

grabs some new ammo, and hands me a pair of earmuffs. He takes me down to the farthest lane, past a couple of stone-faced dudes firing at paper targets.

"Alright," Mace says, his voice loud and gruff enough to penetrate the big orange muffs over my ears. He snaps the black case open and shows me a Browning Hi-Power Practical, this gorgeous .40 caliber semi-auto of black and shiny steel. As soon as I see it, I'm just itching to get my fingers around the grip. I decide to have a little fun and wait patiently as Mace hefts the weapon into his hand and starts explaining things I learned about when I was five years old: how to load the magazine, how to switch off the safety, how to hold and aim.

When he finally hands the gun over to me, I grip it awkwardly and bite my lip, fanning my lashes as I step up to the range and eye the big red and white target at the end of it. With a deep inhale, I lift the gun up in both hands, just the way my daddy taught me, take aim, and then fire off three shots.

The first one hits dead-center and the second two ... go right through the same hole.

I smirk, flick my eyes over to Mace's stunned face, and then finish off the clip before I drop the magazine into my palm and slam in a new one.

"Beginner's luck?" I ask with a raised brow, but Mace has already seen right through me, crossing his arms and watching as I shoot a circle around the target, outlining the big red ring with ten shots before

I have to reload again.

"What else do you know how to do, Talia?" Mace asks, giving me a nickname in the moment. I consider it for a second and decide I'd rather not have any of these other guys hear my real name, just in case.

I activate the safety and set the gun aside, offering up a sly smile.

"You'd be surprised to learn what I can do, Mace-y," I purr, putting one hand on the thick, hard muscles in his arm and giving him a ridiculous nickname that in no way fits his looks or his personality. But it's funny and cute and he lets me say it without bitching or complaining. In fact, the look in his eyes very much says he's enjoying this moment with me.

"Are we talking about combat experience?" he growls as I step closer and look up, up, up into his face. "Or something else?"

"Why don't we head back to your Hummer, and I can show you what we're talking about?" I purr, batting my lashes in a coquette move I perfected years ago. I take another step closer and feel the hard evidence of his interest press against my torso.

Mace looks down at me for a long moment, his lids heavy with blatant lust.

"Are you often like this?" he asks me in a rumbling, quiet voice like a faint earthquake.

"Confident?" I reply, arching a brow at him in challenge.

"Sexual," he corrected, taking a very deliberate step

back from me and causing my jaw to drop. Have I just totally misread those signals? *How?*

I frown. "Wait, you're into me. I can *tell*." I nod pointedly to his thick erection pressing against the fabric of his pants, and he makes no move to try and disguise it.

"I am. You're a gorgeous girl, Talia, and your marksmanship is ..." he trails off with a sexual sounding groan, "but you've been through some bad shit. A blind man could see that you use sex and substances to hide from your reality. Only a real asshole would take advantage of you when you're vulnerable like this, and regardless of my profession, I'm no asshole."

This makes me pause. Stunned. Speechless.

What is he saying about his leader? Surely, he heard Hawke fucking me earlier; we weren't exactly quiet about it. More to the point, what does this say about me that I'm even more attracted to Hawke *because* he's an asshole?

Then again, Mace's refusal of me just makes him a challenge, and I *love* a good challenge. Especially when they come in the form of a six-foot four mountain of hard muscle and sizeable cock. At least, from what I can see through his pants.

"Come on," he smiles, "clearly you don't need any shooting lessons from me today. Do you want to just fire off some AK-47 rounds for the fun of it? Or we can head outside and hit some long-range targets with a Fieldcraft?"

Chewing my lip thoughtfully, I eye him up again to check if he's really sure about turning down my offer. His steady gaze doesn't waver though, so I shrug.

"Sure, long-range sounds good. My sniper skills could use some work anyway seeing as Daddy only really taught me handguns." I hand the weapon back to Mace to put back in his case and stretch out my back. One thing's for sure, the mattresses in the church's sleeping quarters could seriously do with an upgrade. Maybe I could order them some online ...

Ugh, except my father will be watching my credit cards. Yeah, that's a no go.

Great, I'm homeless and broke. How the mighty have fallen, eh Natty?

Mace leads me back out to the hummer, where he lifts a panel in the back to switch his weaponry for something a little larger. He slings the case over his broad shoulder and tosses an easy grin at me.

"I can easily say this is the best date I've ever taken a chick on before," he comments oh so casually as we head through to the outdoor range where several guys are on their bellies as they fire.

"Date?" I squeak in shock.

He sets the rifle case down at an empty spot at the far end and turns to me with a clear challenge in his face. "Yeah. A meal and an activity with a partner you find sexually attractive. That's a date, isn't it?"

My jaw moves, but no sound comes out. I literally

have no clue how to respond to that, and given I've never actually been on a *date* before. Plenty of sex, just ... no real dates.

"But we just met," I whisper as the surprise begins to dissipate a little.

Mace just shrugs, kneeling down to take his weapon out—the rifle, I mean—and gives me a lazy, self-confident smile. "What can I say, Talia? You give quite the first impression. Now, get down here and shoot some shit with me."

"Yes, sir," I murmur, sinking to my knees while still feeling stunned. This enormous weapon of a man is not acting *at all* how I'd come to expect. I can't help but feel intrigued by that ... more than that, his eagerness to be on a *date* with me after he just heard me fucking his boss is astounding. And wildly arousing.

Something tells me I'll enjoy being prisoner to these five fake priests.

7

NATALIA

"So what's the deal with you guys anyway?" I ask Weston across the kitchen table, finally giving into my curiosity. "I know you're not government, and you're *definitely* not clergy. So what are you?"

Weston narrows his cognac colored eyes at me, fiddling with his lip piercing and not answering my question immediately. Instead, he drums the fingers of his left hand on the table and makes me squirm under his intense stare.

"Okay, don't ask?" I guess, shifting uncomfortably in my seat and wishing I could hide under the table or something.

"Tell me something, *Natalia*," he says finally, putting a strange inflection on my name that makes me frown at him in confusion. "You were very vocal during that fucking church service I was running earlier. Might I ask if you had any encouragement in that matter?"

His gaze still holds me captive, and I squirm again awkwardly. My face is flushing with embarrassment, I can already tell, which seems to be all the answer he requires as he nods and *finally* blinks.

"I see." He clicks his top teeth on the metal spearing his lip. "Hawke?" Again, I don't answer vocally, but give him a tiny nod of my head in confirmation.

"Motherfucker," Weston swears, shoving his chair back from the table and pushing a hand through his black and green hair. "I knew it. Excuse me while I go and punch that cunt."

He gives me no more time to form words, even if I had any, before storming out of the kitchen and almost knocking Colt over on his way in.

"Whoa, bro." Colt chuckles, looking after Weston's retreating form. "Where's the fire?"

His mention of fire makes me recall the sight of Kisten burning, and I swallow back a lump of guilt and fear.

When Weston doesn't respond, Colt looks to me with a dirty blond brow raised.

"He said something about going to punch Hawke," I inform him with wide eyes. The last thing I want is to cause in-fighting between my captors. I really, *really* want them all to get along. With and without their clothes.

That might sound a bit presumptuous of me, but there are two key factors driving my actions. One, I was raised to believe I could have anything I wanted in life. I'm the daughter of Konstantin Petrov, Russian mob boss. No one tells me no. And two, my days are numbered.

Anyone might be forgiven for thinking I'm a spoiled, stupid rich girl, but I'm far from stupid. These men are offering me their protection, like they can save me from my fate, but they're only delaying the inevitable. Sooner or later both my father, and my choices, will catch up with me. And when that happens, death will be the best I can hope for.

So yeah, I intend to make the most of my final days of breathing, and anyone who would judge me for that can go straight to hell.

"What's that look for?" Colt asks me, jolting me out of my thoughts. "You look sad."

"Hm?" I blink up at him, struck once again by how handsome he is. With his clear, bottle-green eyes and floppy blond hair, he looks like some sort of Australian surfer or actor.

"Nat," he smirks at me, pulling a chair around the table until he's sitting within touching distance. He's dressed in faded jeans and a white t-shirt that strains across his muscular chest. Not one of these guys could have anything more than two percent body fat to share between them, but I guess that's to be expected from *whatever* they are. Mercenaries? Spies? Regardless, I doubt I'll find any dad bods doing undercover missions that involve my father's affairs.

"Yes, Colt?" I reply sweetly, pushing aside my thoughts of death—or worse—and focusing on the here and now. I haven't forgotten our interrupted fuck earlier, and his close proximity is making that desire resurface.

"What's going on in that pretty head of yours?" He reaches out and strokes a lock of my chestnut hair behind my ear. Internally, I'm rolling my eyes. Phrases like that come across so condescending to any woman with half a brain.

Colt, I'm sure, doesn't mean it like that. I find it hard to believe he's anything less than sincere.

"Just thinking about how we were so rudely interrupted this morning," I respond, flipping my mental flirt switch firmly into the *on* position. Like I said, if I only have days left to live, I want to *fully* enjoy them. Then maybe, before my father can exact a punishment worse than death, I can leave this world on my own terms.

A grin spreads over Colt's handsome face. "It's all I've been able to think about today, too. I hope Weston actually *does* punch Hawke. He fucking deserves it."

His long fingers extract a hand-rolled cigarette from the squashed cardboard pouch he pulls from his pocket. "You don't mind if I smoke, do you?"

"Go for it," I tell him, watching with thinly veiled interest as he flicks his zippo lighter open and touches the end of his cigarette to the flame. The second it's ignited, my suspicion is confirmed and I smile with amusement. "Colt, that's not tobacco."

"No?" He smirks back at me with a wink. "Better remind me to confess this next Sunday."

He takes a long drag on the joint and then offers it to me, which I gratefully accept. It's been more than twenty-four hours since my last glass of champagne and baggy of top quality coke at my father's party. Over twenty-four hours since I saw my lover shot while his hard cock was still buried between my thighs.

"Fuck," I breathe when the heady smoke fills my lungs. "That's some good shit."

Colt grins and winks as I pass it back. "Only the best, Tzarina." He holds my heavy-lidded gaze for a long moment before we hear voices coming down the hall toward the kitchen. It sounds like Hawke and Mace, but Colt shoots out of his seat like it's on fire.

"Quick," he hisses, holding a hand out to drag me from my own seat. Without pausing to explain further, he quickly flings the freezer open and grabs a bottle of liquor before dragging me through a different door and into a dark corridor.

"Colt?" I ask hesitantly, and he shushes me.

"Quiet," he whispers, placing the joint back between my lips in the darkness and tugging me by my hand. "Hawke and Mace get real pissy about me smoking on a job. Which is hypocritical as fuck seeing as they both have their own vices, but whatever. Not worth the argument, you know?"

"Say no more." I cough as I follow him out into the dark church. There're some candles lit, which I imagine were lit all night. But what the hell do I know? I thought this place had a nunnery for fuck's sake, which it very clearly does not.

"Here," Colt murmurs, pulling me into a pew in the middle of the huge structure, shadowed by an ornately carved pillar bearing a heavy wooden cross. We sit on the hard bench, close enough that our thighs press together, and Colt drapes an arm over my shoulders.

The entire church is still, and silent.

"This feels ..." I whisper into the darkness, passing the joint back to him.

"Naughty?" he offers, quirking a brow at me and giving me the truest sense of his character thus far. Colt is the *naughty* one. "Let's make it naughtier." He hands me the bottle he grabbed on our dash out of the kitchen. "Russian, like you."

I snicker, inspecting the label to find it is indeed, Russian vodka. Delicious. Eagerly, I twist the cap off and take a long gulp, feeling the smooth liquid burn a path down my throat and warm my belly.

Fuck yeah. This is exactly how I want to spend my last days.

"How long until Hawke or Mace come looking for us?" I ask Colt quietly, already feeling the haze of pot making my body heavy and slow. It's like being wrapped in cotton wool, which is only heightened by the vodka.

"Long enough," Colt replies, taking the bottle from me and tipping it back for a swallow while holding my gaze. "We can always hide out in the confessional if you're worried they'll find us before we're ready?"

My brows shoot up and excitement zaps through my body. "You actually have a confessional here?"

Colt scoffs. "Tzarina, *all* self-respecting churches have confessionals. Wanna see?"

I grin at his new nickname for me. Tzarina means Empress in Russian, and I kind of love it. "Hell yeah," I accept, taking his hand as he stands.

We walk slowly up the aisle to the front of the church, where Colt puts out the end of his joint in the pool of holy water. Something about that act turns me on exponentially and suddenly I'm dying to be enclosed in a small, *tight* space with Colt.

The confessional itself is set to the side of the church, away from the pews and enclosed with beautifully detailed sliding wooden doors, rather than the curtains I'd expected. Too many low-budget movies have colored my expectation of churches, I guess.

Colt approaches one side of the booth and slides the door open. "After you, Tzarina."

I see the invitation in his eyes, and eagerly accept it by stepping into the small booth and perching on the little bench seat. He follows me in, and I shuffle over as far as possible to make room while he slides the door shut again.

Once inside, Colt solves the problem of space by lifting me up and setting me on his lap. Giggling, I accept the bottle of vodka from him and take a couple more sips before handing it back.

"Now what?" I breathe, and even I can hear the lust in my voice. Even if Colt and I hadn't almost fucked this morning, pot and vodka make me horny as shit. I want him. Bad.

Colt takes another sip himself, then in a low voice commands me, "Get on your knees, Natalia."

I suck in a sharp breath, and don't hesitate even a second before doing as I'm told. My knees hit the hard floor with an audible thump, and I gasp at the sharp pain. I'm no stranger to the sensation—pain, that is—and I love it.

It reminds me I'm still alive ... for now.

"Like this?" I check, peering up at Colt in the darkness. He's still seated on the little bench, his legs spread while I kneel between them, facing him.

"Perfect," he confirms, taking another swig of vodka and then passing the bottle to me.

As I bring the glass rim to my lips, I watch Colt

unbuckle his jeans and withdraw his rigid erection. I'd only grabbed the briefest glimpse of his equipment earlier, before Hawke had interrupted us and thrown Colt out of the room, and I'm simply dying to get better acquainted.

"You owe me a happy ending," Colt tells me sternly, but I can hear the edge of amusement in his voice. "I think you know what to do."

Grinning, I lick my lips and hand the vodka back. I reach out, trailing my fingers down the soft skin of Colt's dick, then grip the base firmly to bring him to my lips. Given I'm on my knees with his cock in my face, it isn't any great leap to work out he wants a blow job. I'm all too happy to give it to him, too.

My vast and varied sex life has given me a great number of nifty skills, and I'm not ashamed to admit that I can suck some seriously great cock. Being able to deep throat is always an advantage, too, which Colt is soon going to learn.

"That's it," he encourages, setting the vodka aside on the bench and bringing his hands to my hair. "Suck me, Tzarina."

I fight a smile as I roll my tongue over the silken head of his cock, tasting the salty pre-cum and relishing in his arousal. My head is spinning from the combination of vodka and pot, and I'm just high enough to feel like a normal girl. Not the daughter of a Russian mob boss, on the run from death and worse, captive at the hands of a gang of mercenaries in a church.

No, right now I'm just a girl, sucking her boyfriend's cock in a confessional.

Colt groans low in his throat as I take him deeper, working my hand around his base as I suck him hard. I'm no amateur, I know what men like—whether they admit it or not—so I carefully but firmly scrape my teeth down his sensitive skin.

He sucks in a sharp breath, but I could swear there's an echo. Like, there's someone else breathing heavily nearby. But then again, maybe it's just weird acoustics inside the little confessional booth messing with my mind. Or the pot.

My other hand slides up, cupping his balls and rolling them gently as he moans his approval. It gives me such a sense of satisfaction, knowing I can have such an effect on someone as hot as Colt.

Again, I hear a noise that pulls me from the moment, like there's someone else present and watching, but before I can pull away to look, Colt fists his hands in my hair and bucks his hips. His hard length slams into the back of my throat, and I have no option but to swallow him deep. It's either that or choke, and I'm not a fan of gagging around cock.

"Holy shit," he swears, using his grip on my hair to roughly dictate pace and depth. It's something a lot of girls hate. That feeling of helplessness, of vulnerability. For me, it's a goddamn turn-on, and I can already feel my panties growing wetter by the second as he fucks my throat.

My hands grip tight to the bench seat beside his thighs, holding on for dear life as he uses me, then grunts his release as he comes. His hot load hits the back of my throat, and I swallow, licking around the length of his dick as he finally releases me and withdraws from my mouth.

"That was exactly what I needed," Colt groans, collapsing back on the bench and tucking his dick away into his jeans. "I've been hard as a rock all damn day. Listening to you and Hawke almost killed me, even if it did tell me something interesting about you."

"Oh?" I arch a brow at him while wiping my mouth off on my sleeve. "What's that?"

Colt leans in close, close enough that his lips brush my ear and I shiver. I'm so turned-on that even that small touch sends shockwaves through me.

"I learned that you love it rough, Tzarina." He pats my cheek teasingly, just this side of a slap. "And you're a goddamn natural submissive. So I think I might leave you worked up like I *know* you are right now. Consider it punishment for torturing me this morning."

Indignation boils, and I open my mouth to protest, but he just lays a finger across my lips to silence me.

"You know you deserve it. Now run along before Hawke finds us and we *both* catch a spanking." He says this with a grin and a wink, and I find myself hesitating, hoping Hawke *does* catch us. Maybe then

I'd get my own happy ending.

But I'm also pissed as hell that Colt is being a dick and not returning the favor, so I purse my lips and push up from the floor. Riding my rage, I snatch up the bottle of vodka and spin on my heel to storm out of the little booth, but as I do, something catches my eye.

There's a wicker mesh screen dividing the two halves of the confessional booth, separating the side Colt and I are in, from the other side, the side where the priest would sit. When we'd entered I'd been fairly sure we were alone, but as I pause, a pair of ice-blue eyes meet mine through the mesh.

Arsen.

He slowly winks one eye, then lays a finger to his lips, indicating I stay quiet about his presence there. And I do.

Don't ask me why, because I can't be bothered trying to rationalize my insane actions of late, but I simply wink back, lick my lips, and leave the booth. The double breathing while I'd sucked Colt off makes sense now, and I almost come just picturing Arsen pleasuring himself while watching us.

He's fucking crazy, that much is well-established. But damn me to hell if I'm not picturing what that crazy might do to me if we were left alone. The thought sends a rush of adrenaline flooding through me, fear and desire warring for supremacy and coming out even.

UNDERCOVER SINNERS

My footsteps echo through the dark church as I wander back to the living quarters, and I take another sip of vodka. The alcohol warms my belly and a grin curves over my face.

If Colt isn't going to finish me off ... I wonder if someone else might?

8

NATALIA

To my disappointment, there's no one in the kitchen when I return, and no sounds of the other guys anywhere nearby. Briefly, I consider escape. But the thought doesn't last long.

I laugh bitterly to myself, draining the last of the vodka and setting it unsteadily on the kitchen counter. Prisoner or not, I'm a hell of a lot safer here than I would be fending for myself. Like I've already said, I'm no idiot.

Wobbling my way up the stairs, I head toward the room that Mace said was mine. It's identical to every other bedroom I've seen so far. Small and sparse with a lumpy single bed and a horror film looking crucifix on the wall.

"Oops," I slur, pausing in the doorway when I

notice someone standing inside. The broad mountain-like shoulders are a dead giveaway. "Mace, I thought … this was my room?"

"It is, Talia," he replies, turning to face me with a small smile. "I just wanted to wish you goodnight." He steps close, towering over me and forcing me to crane my neck to see him.

"That's sweet of you, Macey," I murmur with alcohol numbed lips.

"Hmm," he hums. "We'll see. My bedroom is across the hall, in case you need me."

I squint up at him. "What does that mean?"

The smile he gives me is tight and regretful. "You'll see." He presses a gentle kiss to my lips then swipes a thumb over my cheek. "Good luck, Talia."

He's gone before I can formulate any further questions, leaving me confused and fuzzy. Nothing a bit of sleep can't fix, but first I need to sort out the throbbing arousal between my thighs.

Eagerly, I push my oversized pants down, kicking them into the corner and then tugging my top over my head. Just as it obscures my face, I hear my bedroom door close with a firm click.

"Natalia." Hawke's sharp voice makes me jump, and I spin to face him in nothing but my ill-fitting bra and panties. "You've been drinking."

I nod, then open my mouth to give an excuse, but he beats me to it.

"And smoking pot. With Colt, I presume."

Again, I nod. "Yes, but—"

"Do not speak until I ask you a question." Hawke's words snap through the room like a whip, and I flinch. In a good way. I can already feel my nipples tightening and my breath growing short. I wonder if he'll fuck me again? Maybe if I ask nicely ... "If you're going to be a part of this team, you will follow my orders."

'Who said I want to be a part of your team?" I slur, because this is all happening so fast and hell, an experienced party chick like me knows you shouldn't smoke and then drink. It's supposed to be the other way around. When you smoke first, the alcohol amps up the THC to levels that make you ... well, couch-locked as fuck.

I slump onto the edge of the bed. I'm in a good mood right now, the best I've been in in *years*. Like, I'm too relaxed to care about anything, including myself. I sit there, and it feels like hours before Hawke moves over to the edge of the bed. That's how it works when you're high though, time slows down to immeasurable levels.

"Clearly, you're intoxicated. We'll have this discussion in the morning." Hawke pushes me down onto the bed, and my heart begins to race. I want him on top of me, moving inside of me with his thick cock. Maybe it *would* be worth joining this team, just for all the easy lays? I giggle as I roll toward him and hook my fingers around the waistband of his jeans.

"Like you have any room to talk," I purr, trying to get Hawke to come to me. Instead, he takes a step back, and I frown. Moonlight leaks into the room and stains his face with silver, highlighting the rugged shape of his jaw and the darkness of the stubble tracing his skin. "You've got vices, Colt says so. You and Mace."

Hawke laughs at me, but it's not a particularly pleasant sound. There's a darkness to it that I feel like he'd hide if he could. And I'm intrigued by that. Why am I so damn intrigued? Clearly, there's something broken and twisted inside of me.

"Me and Mace? Please. Weston and Colt are the addicts here. Hard to say if Arsen is or not, he's so damn crazy." Hawke leans down, putting a big palm on my pillow. I can feel the warmth of his body, and I stretch toward it, like a flower toward the sun. A flower that wants to get *fucked* in this bed right here, right now. "Rest up, Natalia Petrova."

"Stay with me," I beg, but Hawke presses a rough kiss to my forehead and steps back. There's something ominous about that kiss, nothing sweet. It's like he's promising dark deeds for later.

"In the morning, we'll *really* get started with your training," he says, retreating from the room and slamming the door behind him. I wonder if he's as aware of how fucked-up his own sexuality is, the way I am. Clearly, Hawke likes to be dominant. He craves it. Even more so than he craves being in control of his team.

You're so full of shit, Talia, I think, rolling onto my back and grinning stupidly at my new nickname. It takes so much effort to roll over that all I can do is *think* about touching my clit, working off some of the wild frenzy in my blood. But I'm moving in a cloud of THC and it's just easier to lie there and count silver stars where one of the ceiling beams connects to the wall. The moon highlights a bunch of those glow in the dark star stickers that some long ago kid must've put up there.

That's how I fall asleep, counting them and letting waves of desire wash over me, unsatisfied and unfettered.

And my dreams? They're full of handsome priests who are not priests, five handsome men in my bed making me submit at the same time they grant me ultimate power over them by handing over their love. It's a serious fairy-tale and unlike anything I've ever dreamed before.

I'm out before I get a chance to think too hard about it.

I'll be dead before anything like that ever happens.

Several hours later, I wake up, still high but measurably more functional.

UNDERCOVER SINNERS

"Jesus fucking Christ," I snap as I sit up and my head spins like I'm on the tilt-a-whirl at the county fair. It was so fun, that one time I went. But then I saw Daddy shoot a man, his wife, and their teenage son for failing to pay a debt. I puked up all of my cotton candy and never set foot in a fairground again.

"Now is that any way to talk in a *church*?" a voice asks, snapping my eyes up to the heavy wood beams in the vaulted ceiling. Arsen is *sitting* on one of them, and I'm still too fucked-up to puzzle out why. Instead, I just squint and do my best to push myself up to my feet.

"I need some water," I groan, because I've got the worst of both worlds: dry mouth from the pot and a hangover from all that booze.

"Water? Is that really what you need?" he asks, sliding off the edge of the beam and hanging briefly from it for a moment before he drops to his feet in front of me. Arsen's ice-blue eyes take me in from head to toe, and it's only when I see the fire in his gaze that I realize I'm naked. *When did that happen?* "Because I might have something else you're interested in."

He reaches out and grabs my hand, putting my palm on his bare chest. He's not wearing anything but a pair of black sweatpants, his tattoos blue-gray and brilliant in the moonlight. My sluggish brain catches on the designs and just flat-out refuses to let go. Underneath my hand, I can hear his heart beating.

"You have a heart," I say, and he raises a single brow at me.

"Do I now?" he asks, sliding my hand over to the peaked point of his nipple. "I guess I needed *something* inside of me to pump all that blood to my cock. Lord knows it's not useful for much else."

I don't have a lot of inhibitions on a normal day, so when I'm high and slightly hungover? I end up pinching and teasing Arsen's nipple, drawing this ragged sound from his throat.

"I need water," I repeat again after moment, pushing past him and heading for the door. I stumble down the stairs and he follows after me. When I get to the bottom, I find one of the guys' robes lying across the small table near the coffee maker and pick it up, slinging it over my shoulders.

In the kitchen, I find a chipped coffee mug and fill it three times over with cool water from the tap, gasping as I lean over the old farmhouse sink and try not to throw up. Why didn't I just stick to the pot? The pot never makes me sick like this.

When I finally do stand up and turn around, I find Arsen leaning against the larger table, his arms crossed over his chest as he watches me like I'm one of the most fascinating things he's ever seen. And when I say *things*, I mean things. He doesn't look at me like I'm a woman or even a person. I try not to take it personally; he looks at his fellow team members like that, too.

"Can I help you with something?" I finally ask, leaning my ass against the counter and breathing in the smell of the robes I just borrowed. They have the faintest whiff of pot and something else, this musky male scent that reminds of ... Weston? Not like I've spent more than two seconds with the guy, but when I close my eyes and breathe in that smell, he's the one that first comes to mind.

"Something?" Arsen asks, lighting up a cigarette right there in the kitchen. "I thought you wanted to fuck? I waited for Hawke to go to bed and then climbed out my window and into yours." He shrugs his broad shoulders, silver-gray smoke drifting around his face as he watches me through the haze, like a lion stalking its prey. "I hate your family and everything they stand for. So, by association, I hate you, too. If I didn't think Hawke would kill *me*, I might kill you instead. As things stand, I'd rather we just screwed each other."

He says it so matter-of-fact. Like he's talking about drinking tea instead of coffee. He'd *rather* coffee, but he'd settle for tea.

I continue to sip my water, the long dark sleeves of the robes falling over my hands as I gaze across the chipped rim over to Arsen and his pretty boy face. He's too beautiful to be so crazy, too damaged to be gorgeous. And yet, I find that I can't look away.

"Okay," I say after a moment, setting my drink aside.

Arsen raises a single brow at me, but he doesn't stop smoking his cigarette, holding it between two inked fingers as I take a step closer to him. He's so still for so long that I start to wonder if the pot's still messing with my brain.

In the blink of an eye though, he's tossing his smoke into the sink and grabbing me, shoving me face first over the surface of the table and pushing the robes up around my bare hips. No words pass between us as Arsen shoves his sweats down and then finds my opening with the slick tip of his cock.

He shoves his way into me and I scream, clutching at the edges of the table as I'm filled up and stretched to the edge of my usual limits. Wow. Of *course* the crazy man would be the one to be packing.

My nails curl into the wood of the table as Arsen pauses to light up another cigarette—I can't see him, but I can smell it, can hear the flick of his lighter. He holds the smoke between his lips, grips my pelvis with a bruising hand on the left side. His fingers tangle in my hair, yanking hard enough that I let out a small whimper.

The sex between us is rough, messy, and broken. It highlights everything wrong in both me and him. We're not using protection; we didn't even talk about it. We don't know each other. We don't like each other. I'm high, and he's crazy, and we shouldn't be doing this.

But it feels so damn good.

Arsen pumps into me hard and fast, pulling zero punches as he goes balls-deep. He isn't gentle or careful when he pulls my hair and drives into me, doesn't care about boundaries or shared pleasure. He just *takes*. I let him do it, too, thrust into me so hard that I know I'll have bruises on the front of my pelvis come morning.

My moans are ragged and broken as Arsen speeds up his movements and comes with a harsh, rough sound, spilling himself inside of me and pulling away abruptly. He leaves me cold and wet and pulsing, my empty inner walls aching to clench down on something, on someone.

"That was ... interesting," he says, smoking his cigarette as he yanks up his sweats and retreats around the table. I watch him go, listening to his feet on the stairs. And then ... I turn and head for the door that leads outside, ripping it open and making a run for it while I have the chance.

9

NATALIA

The grass is wet and dewy under my feet as I sprint across the churchyard and toward the sidewalk. I have no idea where I'm going, but my emotions are suddenly mixed up, so twisted that I can't seem to see straight anymore. Cum leaks down my thighs as I run, but I don't care, I just keep going until I find myself at a playground six blocks away.

That's about when it hits me, that I have no money, nowhere to go, no family except for the father that pointed his gun at the chest of a man who was still inside of me. I sink down to the ground, huddled inside the robes and then collapse against the side of a green bench, folding my arms atop it and resting my forehead against them.

It feels like I'm trapped, and I don't want to be

trapped. For the first time in my life, what would it be like if I were free?

"I come here every once in a while to think," a voice says, drawing my head up. I see Weston with his wild green hair and piercings sitting on the next bench over. How I missed him, I have no idea, but all I really want to say is *teach me*. When he stands up and walks toward me, his footsteps make no sound. "Are you leaving?"

"Will you try to stop me if I say yes?" I ask as Weston takes a seat on my bench and looks down at me with his dark eyes. He doesn't look sympathetic, but he also doesn't look like he's judging me either. I like that. I sit up and haul myself onto the bench. My feet are now mucky and wet, and my thighs are slick with Arsen's cum. All I want to do right now is slink back to the church, hope Hawke didn't notice me missing, and climb into the shower.

"No," Weston says, surprising me. He's wearing faded jeans and an old band t-shirt that's so old I can't quite read the name of the band anymore. "If you want to leave, I certainly won't keep you." He stares straight ahead, across the street at a row of historic homes, all lovingly restored with big wide porches. There's a split-second there where I wish I lived in one of them, so I could sleep in a king size bed in silky Victoria's Secret pajamas and cuddle up to a husband, get up and have coffee and toast with him.

Like that'll ever happen for me.

"Do you want coffee and toast?" I ask when I can't think of anything else to say. It's super fucking embarrassing to have a breakdown you think you're alone for, only to find out someone's been watching all along.

His brow quirks and a small smile pulls up the corner of his pierced lip. "I don't know if we have any bread at the church, but we could go pick some up? It's about damn time we refilled the fridge anyway." I rub my thighs together, trying to figure out some way to tell Weston that I'm not quite fit to go shopping at the moment when he seems to read my mind. "I've got some spare sweats in my car if you don't want to go back to the church?"

I give him a small, embarrassed smile. "That'd be great, thank you."

Weston says nothing more, just shrugs and leads the way out of the playground and down the block, stopping beside a sleek black Dodge Challenger. He pops the trunk and pulls out a pair of grey sweatpants and a black hoodie with frayed cuffs.

"Here," he holds them out to me, "they'll be huge, but probably better than running around in a clergy robe."

"Thanks," I whisper, accepting the garments then looking around awkwardly. Am I supposed to just strip down here in the street? I'm no stranger to nudity, but this is a bit much for public scrutiny.

"Change in the car, idiot," Weston snickers, pulling

the passenger side door open for me and ushering me in. Blushing, I take the offered seat and let him close the door firmly behind me.

The windows are tinted dark enough that I feel no shame stripping the billowy black robe off my naked flesh. Until the driver's door opens and Weston climbs inside that is.

"Um," I hesitate, half-heartedly covering my breasts with the cloth of his hoodie.

"Problem?" He challenges me with a quirk of his pierced brow. "You don't strike me as the shy type, Natalia."

I snort a laugh. "You're right, I'm not." It must be the lingering effects of pot and alcohol that're making me bashful. Weston is fucking hot, and I know full well how great my tits are, so why am I covering them?

With a shrug, I drop the black fabric and allow him an unobstructed view of my full breasts and tight pink nipples. He takes the opportunity, too, sucking in a breath and catching his lip ring between his teeth while I dress ever so slowly.

When I'm done, he makes a noise somewhere between a scoff and a laugh. "You sure do know your own power, Natalia. I fucking hope Hawke knows what he's doing, bringing you onboard."

I grin at the compliment. "Are we going grocery shopping or what?"

"Yes ma'am," he replies, giving me a sly grin and

starting up his engine.

We don't speak again for the few minutes it takes to get to the grocery store, and when we arrive Weston opens my door for me. Manners I didn't really expect from someone with so many pieces of metal in his flesh. Is that a stereotype? Probably. But I'm a rich party-girl daughter of a mobster, so I think I'm allowed to stereotype sometimes.

"You know," he murmurs close to my ear as we cross the parking lot, "those nipples of yours would look great pierced."

I gasp at the suggestion, but before I can respond, I hear heavy footsteps behind us.

I don't have to be a genius to know that nothing good will come from that sound.

Weston stiffens up and glances casually over his shoulder.

"Hey man," he says, just before the barrel of a gun is being pointed at the side of his head. I'm pretty sure I'm about to see his brains splattered across the pavement when, in a lightning quick movement, he knocks the man's arm aside and breaks it. I can hear the snap of bone as I jump backwards, almost tripping on the too long sweats.

The man screams and his gun skitters across the asphalt while Weston follows up with a swift fist to his face, once, twice, three times. Blood sprays across the soccer-mom van we're standing beside, and the man's head drops unconscious to the ground.

"Weston!" I scream a warning, split-seconds before another gun is pressed to the back of his head by our attacker's friend. A man I recognize all too well.

My blood runs cold, and I fight the urge to vomit.

They found me. How have they found me, so soon?

I'm screwed.

My mind is working a million miles an hour as one of my father's men, Dmitri, leers at me with a triumphant grin.

He sneers something to me, but my mind doesn't comprehend it. It's fight or flight time, and I am *not* ready to give up. Not on their terms.

I dart my eyes around, and spot the gun dropped by the other man. It's under the next car over, too far from where I stand.

I dive for it anyway, a gunshot lighting up the dark night as I skid across the pavement and roll, my fingers curling around the grip of the gun just before I get a boot to the back. My spine curves in agony and my mouth opens in a silent scream. The gun is still in my hand, but whoever it is that's standing behind me doesn't let up, kicking me again and again and again, until the pain is so great that my fingers uncurl around the weapon and it drops back to the pavement.

"Your father is mighty disappointed in you, Natalia," Dmitri says, dragging me out from under the car and lifting me up with a fistful of fabric. He slams me into the trunk of a nearby car, the streetlamps painting his face orange as he smiles at me. It's an icy, cold smile, the smile of a total psychopath. There's nothing in that man's face that says he ever was or would ever be human. This is the same man who killed his own wife in cold-blood for watching porn. So what the fuck is he going to do to me?

The last thing in the world I'd ever want is to find out the answer to that question.

I throw my knee up as hard as I can, nailing Dmitri in the crotch, but whereas a normal man might scream or howl or let go of me, all that move does is get the crazy psycho to laugh. I can't see Weston, but the dark parking lot is quiet now. There are no more gunshots, no screaming bystanders, no distant police sirens.

We're all alone out here, in a pre-dawn dark parking lot outside a shitty market with hand-drawn sales signs in the windows. This is *not* the place or the way I will die.

Since Dmitri is still holding me up by the front of Weston's hoodie, I drop down and slide out of it. It's so loose that it comes right off, and I'm blessed with a few precious seconds to lunge for the gun. The pain of my bare nipples and breasts scraping across the pavement when I lunge ... Well, nobody can ever say I'm not at least a *little* bit of a badass.

I roll onto my back as Dmitri grabs my ankle and yanks me toward him, firing off a shot that hits him right in the ear, blood spraying across the trunk of the car he just threw me up against.

"You fucking bitch!" he screams, whipping his own

gun from a holster inside his jacket. There's zero hesitation when he lines it up to take a headshot. I have good aim, so I fight to get my round out first, planning to nail him dead center in the skull.

Instead, a body smashes into Dmitri's, knocking him to the pavement. *Weston!* I think as I scramble back to my feet, my breasts bleeding from my heroic dive. But it's not Weston that's wrestling with my father's favorite assassin: it's *Arsen*. Who better to fight a psychopath than a sociopath, right?

I flick my eyes around the parking lot and spot the green-haired faux priest bleeding on the ground next to his car. Several men are lying still around him. He might be down, but he took several others out with him. I'm torn between whether to stay here and give backup to Arsen or see if there's anything I can do for Weston. As I'm making my decision, one of the men rises to his feet and stumbles against the hood of the Challenger. When he lifts up his weapon, I have a single instant to take action.

Lifting my gun, I let out a long, slow exhale and pretend that I'm back at the shooting range with Mace, aiming at a paper target.

Only this paper target has hair and eyes, and I know for a fact that he's got a family and a name. I've met this man before, and he's only ever been nice to me. But he *is* my father's man, and he'll kill me in instant if those are his orders. I have to be as ruthless if I want to survive. If my father taught me anything all these years, it's that.

I'm going to have *to become a nun after this; surely I'm going to hell.*

I line my aim up and fire off a single shot, hitting the man directly in the side of the head and dropping him before he gets a chance to kill Weston. I just sacrificed the life of one of my father's best men for a guy I don't even know.

Shit, shit, shit.

Arsen rises up from the tangle of arms and legs on the ground and spits blood at Dmitri, whipping out a knife from his belt and spinning it around his fingers. The way he looks at the other man ... I'd piss my pants if I were Dmitri. When I lift my borrowed weapon to focus on my father's right-hand man, Arsen puts up a palm and stops me.

"They talk better when they're alive," he purrs, flicking the blade with two fingers and sinking it into Dmitri's hand when he goes for a second gun on his belt. Arsen steps forward and promptly removes that, lowering the barrel and shooting the man in the thigh.

His scream is awful, but as soon as I hear it, I think of his wife and how she never even got the chance to scream. There's no sympathy left in me after that.

But God, there's so much blood, and it smells so awful. Memories of that night, just a few short days ago, flood my head. Kisten's hard cock buried inside of me, coke and sex and alcohol flooding my blood ... until I'm spattered with his.

UNDERCOVER SINNERS

Clamping a hand over my mouth, I stumble around the side of the soccer-mom van and throw up in a nearby trash can, hooking my fingers around the edges and coughing on the acrid taste poisoning my mouth and throat.

"Here," a deep voice says, and I look up to see Hawke, holding out my abandoned hoodie. My eyes widen as he narrows his and tosses the sweater at me, moving past me and around the van to stare at Dmitri's now still and silent form.

"Are you alright?" Mace asks as he speeds by, heading straight for Weston. I nod briefly, and he grunts, watching as I pull the fabric over my head and join the leader of this motley crew next to the comatose form of one of the evilest men I've ever met in my life. Pretty sure my father is the only person I know who exceeds Dmitri's cruelty. Because while I'm pretty sure that the man lying on the ground in front of me has some severe mental instabilities, my dad has a heart. He lost it when my mother was killed, and he's decided not to bother seeking it out. He *does* feel, and he *does* understand human emotion and pain; he does all the awful things he does in spite of that.

"Start cleaning up," Hawke grunts as the Hummer pulls around and Colt gets out, leaving the engine rumbling. "Not you," he barks, grabbing Colt's arm and turning him around to face me.

"You want me to take the Tzarina back to the church?" Colt asks as I start to shake. Not from fear though. And that's the part that scares me the most, that I'm *not* scared. No, I feel invigorated, adrenaline coursing through my veins with no outlet. That's where the shaking's coming from.

"Make sure you're not being followed," Hawke snaps as Arsen lifts Dmitri's body from the pavement like he's a sack of trash that needs to be taken out. Casually, he tosses him over his shoulder and moves over to the Hummer, opening the back and unceremoniously tossing the man inside.

"No shit, Sherlock," Colt murmurs, rolling his eyes in a dramatic fashion that's clearly meant for me. "Does that mean I get to take West's car?" He grins as he trots around the front of the vehicle and heads toward Mace and Weston.

I'm almost afraid to follow. Colt and Weston seem so close and at this point, I'm not even sure that the latter is still alive …

Swallowing my emotions down, I take a cue from my father and bury my feelings for later—or for good, really—and follow after him. I'm surprised to find Weston standing and drinking from a bottle of whiskey. Really *nice* whiskey, actually.

"Should've known better," Colt says, smiling and patting his friend on the back. He takes the booze from him and drinks from it, not caring that there's a bit of his Weston's blood smeared on the rim. As soon as he finishes grabbing a few swallows, he passes it over to me, and I feel this sense of kinship between the men that makes me envious as hell. They've got something that works here, something that's better than blood, than family, than friendship. I've had all of those things in the past and they've never lasted.

This, what these guys have, it's so much better than that.

A team.

They're a team.

"Five against one? This was so unfair ... for them," Colt finishes as I chug the whiskey and pass it to Mace. He sets it on the trunk of Weston's car and then leans down to pick up the body of the man I shot and killed, throwing him and then *another* man over each shoulder. He seems to have zero problem picking them both up and carrying them to the back of the Hummer; he's not even breathing hard. "Oh, by the way, Hawke says I get to take your car."

"Like hell you do," Weston coughs out, spattering a bit more blood onto the front of his already wet t-shirt. His voice is low and husky with pain. "You drive like a goddamn maniac; there's a reason you no longer have a car of your own. I'll drive."

"We need to get you over to see Portia—" Colt starts and then pales when Weston's gaze snaps over to his face, wild and unhinged. "Shit, shit, shit, I didn't meant to say that."

"No shit," Weston growls out, sagging against the trunk and knocking the whiskey bottle to the ground. I pick it up before it can all spill onto the pavement, mixing with the blood of the dead. Portia, huh? Who the hell is Portia? "Take me back to the church, and I'll patch myself up." West looks like a deflated balloon as he digs in his pocket and hands his keys over to his friend.

I have to bite my tongue to keep from asking about this Portia person. Whoever she was, she must've been pretty goddamn important to elicit such a reaction from Weston. He's got that chill, easygoing vibe about him.

Quietly, I climb into the backseat of the car and wait for the two men to join me.

The song that plays on the way back to the church … is *Bodies* by Drowning Pool.

How appropriate.

10

ARSEN

There's something so infuriating about having Konstantin Petrov's daughter in the same building as me. It's like a slap in the face. Nobody seems to care that I'm here for one reason and one reason alone: to kill that son of a bitch.

    The money is nice, of course, but I don't really give two shits about 'nice things'. Mostly, I'm happy with a bottle of Jack, some cigarettes, and chocolate. Oh yes, I'm a huge fan of chocolate. If my body didn't demand sex, I'd probably be just fine without that, too. It feels good, but it involves being around other people.

Frankly, I'd rather masturbate.

"You sure this girl isn't feeding information to her father?" I ask, and Hawke slams his mug on the counter. He hates talking to me, but I love bothering him, so he best get the fuck over it. "Just seems weird that Weston and Princess Petrova would just *happen* to be jumped the first and only night that West's ever left the church by himself like that."

"The Petrov Syndicate knows where they last saw Natalia, knows that she left on foot, and knows that we're in the area looking for them. It's not much of a stretch to think somebody caught sight of either her or Weston while they were driving and followed them."

I clench my teeth. Sometimes, I wonder how good it would feel to drive a blade through the back of Hawke's neck and watch the pointed end stick out of his throat. He's so rational most of the time, it makes me feel even more insane, the business of my mind spiraling out and around me until it feels like I'm strangling myself.

But I know from Portia that there's more to Hawke than he shows the world.

In the bedroom, he's as dark in the heart and soul and cock as I am.

"I don't like living in the same *dwelling* as that bitch," I say, even though my cock stirs at the thought of her. Fucking that girl did *not* free me from my sudden and inescapable fascination with her; it only made things worse. "If you'll recall, it was *her* father that killed Portia—"

"If you don't shut your goddamn fucking trap ..." Hawke starts, whirling around and sloshing coffee all over the floor.

"Do you two always fight?" a low, husky voice asks from behind me. I don't turn around to look at Natalia. Why bother? If I do, all I'll be able to think about are her bare breasts, bruised and bleeding, that gun clutched in her hands, the way her caramel brown eyes darkened as she took aim at that sack of shit I stabbed.

"We have a love-hate relationship," I lie, shrugging loosely and stretching my arms above my head. "Mostly it's skewed toward hate, but don't tell Hawke that." The leader of our little mercenary troupe gives me a look, but I ignore him. Slowly, carefully, I steel myself to see that woman dressed in oversized robes or sweats or ...

But when I turn and see her wearing one of the old-fashioned nun's habits from the dusty upstairs attic, my cock springs to life. I'm wearing loose acid wash jeans today and nothing else, so it's pretty obvious that I'm turned-on. Natalia notices right away and swallows hard, flicking her eyes to my face.

Does she see how much I despise her? I rightfully *should've* killed her in the bathroom that first day.

Crossing my arms over my chest, I give her a once-over, her brunette hair tucked back under a black and white hood. I'd love to curl my fingers in that fabric and shove her to her knees, get her to suck my cock in the confessional the way she did for Colt.

"Natalia," Hawke says in a strangled sounding voice. It makes me laugh, seeing him so affected by this piece of tits and ass, just like the rest of us. Not even Portia managed to get him to show emotion around the team. "Why are you dressed in that? Didn't Mace buy you some clothes to wear?"

The woman in front of me simply shrugs and runs her tongue over her lower lip. Does she mean it to be suggestive? All I can think about is ramming my dick down her throat now.

"He did, but they don't fit well. Besides, you all get to play dress up as priests. Why can't I play, too?" She arches a brow at Hawke, tilting her chin up defiantly and showing off the creamy pale skin of her neck.

I picture my hands wrapped around it. My fingertips digging in deep, deep enough to bruise as I cut off her air. The mental image is so strong I can hear my breathing speed up, my cock so hard in my pants it's like I'm going to burst my zipper.

"Arsen," Hawke snaps, and I notice both he and this ... *temptress* are watching me intensely. "Give us a few minutes alone."

Regaining a little of my composure—or rather, as much composure as I ever have given how crazy I am—I turn to leer at my *leader*. "Why? So you can bend her over and fuck her tight little cunt right here on the kitchen table? Bad luck, Donald Duck. Been there and done that. This morning, to be precise."

UNDERCOVER SINNERS

My words strike the chord I'm looking for and Hawke's nostrils flare with anger. Shit, pissing him off is almost as good as spilling my seed inside little Miss Petrova was. Seeing her run from me afterwards was a turn-on all by itself, and I had to force myself not to chase her.

"Arsen," Hawke says with careful precision, and I know he's on the edge of snapping. "Get. Out. You have your assignment for the day, now go and do it."

He means the shitty surveillance task he's assigned to me. It's a crock of shit, and so clearly aimed at keeping me away from Miss Petrova. Futile, really. She's piqued my interest, and I sincerely doubt I'll be done with her until one of us is dead.

"As you wish, oh mighty commander Hawke." I tip my imaginary hat at him, then run my eyes over the sexy-as-sin nun's habit concealing Natalia's body. I wonder if she's naked under all that cloth. We'll have to find out later, when Hawke the killjoy isn't around to ruin things.

"I'll be seeing you around, Miss Petrova." I wink at her, not bothering to hide the mix of hatred and lust I'm feeling. I want to kill her just as badly as I want to fuck her. It's quite the conundrum.

She meets my eyes boldly, and I recognize the look in hers. This girl has a death wish, there's no doubt about it. Perhaps we can come to an agreement that we'll *both* find satisfactory ...

Images of sex and death skitter across my mind as I

saunter out of the kitchen, leaving that little minx in Hawke's care while I head out to the cars. Asshole that I am, I snake the keys to Weston's Challenger on my way out. That poisonous girl has me hard as a damn rock and surveillance is a long and boring job. May as well rub one out inside Weston's car and kill two birds with one stone.

Chuckling to myself, I slide into the driver's seat and slam the door shut. I don't bother with a seat belt, because fuck knows it'll take more than a car crash to take me out of the game. Instead, I flick open the fly of my jeans and bare my naked dick while gunning the engine.

Fuck waiting until I get to my assigned location. I can multitask like a pro. I'll sort myself out while I drive.

Tires squealing, I peel out of the parking garage and into the street, merging with traffic seamlessly. Of course, the cunts on the road freak out thinking I'm going to cause an accident and start laying on their horns. Pussies. I'm nowhere near hitting them.

I weave Weston's car between traffic one-handed. My other hand is wrapped firmly around my shaft, pumping up and down as I picture Natalia's mouth on me just like I'd seen her do in the confessional booth. Fucking Colt, that lucky son of a bitch. I've never been so glad to have my quiet time interrupted before.

Just as I'm about to come, I slam on the brakes to avoid rear-ending the truck stopped in front of me.

UNDERCOVER SINNERS

I've pulled up just inches from his tail, and I come hard all over Weston's steering wheel.

Hot, sticky white semen drips down the hand-stitched leather, and I *know* he's never getting it out. Not truly. It makes me laugh. Serves him damn right for getting shot in the first place.

Grabbing the discarded priest robe off his passenger seat, I clean up my dick then tuck it away as traffic begins to move again and my phone rings.

"Arsen," Mace's voice sounds when I answer, but I don't say anything. Why bother? They called me. They know who I am. "We're almost out of iodine and gauze. Can you pick some up on your way back?"

I snort a laugh. "That fuckwit still refusing to see the new doc, eh?"

Mace sighs down the phone. "Yeah. Not that I can blame him. Portia was ..."

He trails off with a wussy noise, and I roll my eyes. Portia was technically a psych nurse, but also became our team's unofficial doctor. Can't just go rocking up to the hospital with gunshot wounds, now can you?

"Yeah, whatever. I'll be back after dark." I don't bother waiting for another response before ending the call.

Bunch of fucking pathetic assholes, my *team* is. Every last one of them, still moping around about a chick that's been dead over a year. Not me, though. I never loved her. Not like they all claimed to. Then again, maybe that's because I'm incapable of love?

ALTERED BY FIRE

Portia certainly thought so. Never stopped her fucking me like her life depended on it though ... and sometimes it did.

Her death was a shock, given it wasn't at my hands, despite how many close calls we'd had while we fucked. No, instead it was at Konstantin Petrov's hands. And for that, I'd see him dead.

Having his prize possession, his little princess, fall into our laps was just the most incredible luck. Perhaps I won't kill her straight away. Perhaps, if I play this stupid game Hawke wants me to play ... make the little bitch *love me* ... it'll make the win all the sweeter.

A cruel sort of grin curves across my lips as I settle into my seat for five hours of surveillance on a damn dry cleaners. Yes, by the time I'm done with Miss Petrova, she will be my loyal and willing slave.

11

NATALIA

Balancing the tray on one hand and my knee, I knock lightly on Weston's door, then push it open gently. Inside, Mace is looming over Weston, mopping up blood from his chest while Colt paces back and forth at the foot of the bed.

"Hey," I say in a soft voice. "Hawke told me to bring this stuff up?"

I hesitate a moment in the doorway, feeling like I'm intruding. These men, they're a team, *a family*. Except for Arsen, that is.

Three sets of eyes snap up to stare at me, and I

ALTERED BY FIRE

freeze to the spot like a deer in the damn headlights. Why?

Get it together, Natty! You're not this shy girl, not outside the bedroom. Chin up, show them you're made of tougher stuff.

"Shall I just leave it here?" I ask, ignoring their stares and carrying the tray over to the small dresser. I need to push aside a bible and a wax candle statue of the Virgin Mary to make space, but once I've done that, I spin to face my audience. "Can I help with something else?"

I intend the question to sound snappy and sarcastic, but for all my best intentions it simply comes out breathy and sexual. Like a slave begging to please her masters.

That inflection doesn't seem lost on the men either, as their gazes turn a little more predatory, and I shift uncomfortably. Not because I don't appreciate their interest, but because now I'm horny as fuck and totally naked under my habit.

It might seem like an odd choice, going without underwear, but I'm dirty as fuck, and it turned me on. So I did it.

"That's all, thank you, Talia." Mace is the first to speak, his voice low and gruff.

"Nice ... outfit?" Colt smirks at me, running his tongue across his lower lip in an undisguised sexual way. "Wearing anything under that?"

Damn him, how did he know?

My thighs clench, and I suck in a deep breath before attempting to reply. "Not a thing," I purr back, then mentally kick myself.

Seriously, Natty? Weston is lying there bleeding from a bullet wound and you're trying to proposition three men at once? One of whom is lying there bleeding? Ugh!

Fuck it. I've got issues. Who gives a rat's ass?

"Actually, Talia," Mace interjects with a cough. "We could maybe use some help. How are your needlework skills?"

"Uh," I hesitate, a bit confused at the change of pace. "Pretty good, actually. Daddy wanted me to be an 'accomplished young woman', so I had to learn all those bullshit sexist 'skills' like sewing, singing, piano ..." I was rambling because my mind had just connected the dots on why they would need needlework. "Uh ah. No way, I'm not stitching up Weston's *flesh*. Are you kidding me? I'm not qualified for that!"

Weston barks a harsh coughing laugh then groans. "It's either you or this asshole." He nods towards Mace. "And I dunno if you've seen those sausages he calls fingers, but they sure don't look nimble to me."

Mace holds up his fingers to show me and damn it if Weston doesn't have a point. Mace's hands are enormous; I'd be amazed if he could even hold a needle.

"What about Colt?" I flail. "His hands are smaller."

"Hey!" Colt objects. "I'll have you know—"

"Colt can't do it," Weston cuts him off. "He gets squeamish around blood. That's why he's down there and not looking at me."

I arch a brow at Colt, and he just shrugs. A faint blush stains his cheeks, so I guess it must be true. But how inconvenient for a mercenary to be squeamish around blood?

Looking between the three men, I find myself nodding before my better judgement can take over. "Okay fine. But don't expect it to be pretty."

Mace lets out a heavy sigh of relief and scoots out of the way for me. Without his huge body obscuring the view, I can clearly see the raw wound in the top of Weston's shoulder, and I too, sigh with relief.

"Oh," I nod. "That's not so bad. That's just a flesh wound, right? Here I was thinking he got shot in the chest."

Mace shakes his head and gives me a small smile. "No, just through the muscle. We still can't take him to the ER though, you know?"

"Still can't believe you got shot and didn't fucking say anything until we got back here, you assface," Colt mutters, spearing Weston with a glare then paling and turning away.

"Can we, maybe, get the fuck on with this?" Weston grimaces, giving me a pleading look. "If that's okay, Natalia? I'm just bleeding a lot here …"

"Oh, right. Yeah. Um." I look around and find Mace

setting up the tray I brought beside the bed. On it is a bowl of warm water and some cloth strips. They already have a wicked looking needle out and threaded with what looks like fishing twine or something, so I guess I'm good to start.

Taking the seat Mace vacated, I scoot a little closer to the bed and take a better look. It's a furrow through his trapezoid about a quarter inch wide where the bullet must have just grazed him, rather than penetrating. Curious, I reach out and pinch the two sides together, just to make sure they reach, and Weston curses.

"Sorry," I mutter, giving him a tight smile. "Not used to working with living fabric, you know?"

"It's fine," he grunts. "Just get it done."

Biting my lip, I dip one of the rags in the water and use it to clean off his skin a little better. I take the needle between my fingers and place it against the side of the wound, considering what type of stitch I should be using. Maybe a blanket stitch? It's kind of like a raw fabric edge, right? No, that won't work ... Overcast stitch is probably the way to go here.

I pause, then position the needle from the other side, but the angles are all wrong from where I'm sitting. It'll need a decent amount of force to pierce flesh, which I won't be able to do from where I'm seated.

"What's wrong?" Weston asks me gruffly, his face pale and sweating.

"The angles aren't right," I admit. "Do you mind if I … um …"

He raises a pierced brow at me. "Just do whatever you need to do, Natalia. Get on with it."

Nodding, I take his permission and climb onto the bed to straddle him. This way, I'm front on to the injury and able to access both sides of the wound with equal force.

Weston grunts, shifting my weight a little until I'm not crushing him so badly, then gives me a tight nod to get started.

"Way better nurse than you," Colt whispers to Mace, but I try to block them out. It's bad enough that I'm about to stitch a man's flesh back together, but I've just realized I'm straddling Weston's bare midsection with absolutely nothing between us. My habit still covers me, but between my legs it's just my bare pussy pressed against Weston's rock-hard abs.

He, too, is aware of this, and I feel him hardening beneath my ass.

"I'm … I'm starting now, okay?" I whisper in a voice that's husky and drenched with desire. Damn my rampant sex drive; now is not the time.

Weston puts his hands on my hips and pushes me down a little further, scooting the blankets out of our way as he goes, until I feel the hard, thick length of his shaft between my cheeks. The ones on my face burn red as West turns his dark eyes over to his companions.

"Get out," he says, and I look over just in time to see Colt open his mouth in protest. "No, don't speak, get the fuck out."

"Screw you, man," Colt starts, but Weston narrows his brown eyes and grits his teeth.

"I'm fucking bleeding to death!" he roars as I hear the door open behind me. Mace is already on his way out, casting a look at me that I just happen to catch. It says *I'm here if you need me*, and it's cute as hell, but ... I wouldn't be doing this if I didn't want to. I might have eclectic tastes in the bedroom, but it's always my choice whether or not I participate in them.

And I so want to participate in this.

"You pulled this same damn shit with Portia," Colt starts, and the look he gets from his friend sends him to his feet, cursing and storming out the door. He slams it behind him, rattling the old walls and knocking a metal crucifix to the floor.

I turn back to Weston and meet his strong gaze, watching as he plays with the piercings in his lip.

"How can I earn the story of Portia?" I ask, and West goes ridiculously still, almost like he's stopped breathing altogether. His brown eyes shift to the side as he exhales.

"Stitch me," he whispers, voice husky and low. "If you do a good job, I'll think about it." He turns back to me with a gravely serious expression etched into his fine features. He has a more delicate jaw and a smaller brow than Colt, but he's just as masculine, just as handsome. "Do not *ever* ask Hawke or Arsen about her though, okay?"

"Okay," I whisper, wiggling back against his cock and getting this low, half-pained growl in response. "But are you sure you only want me to stitch you up?" I wiggle again, and West's hands clamp down hard on my hips. His face is all sweaty, his dark green hair plastered to his forehead, but there's nothing wrong with the rigid length of his cock.

"If that's all I wanted ..." he begins, spearing me with a harsh look at the same time I lift up off his lap and push my already slick pussy back against the head of his dick. "Then I wouldn't have asked Mace and Colt to leave."

As soon as I'm in place, Weston pushes my hips down and impales me on his shaft, drawing this pathetic little mewling sound from my throat. Blood bubbles up and out of the wound on his shoulder, crimson liquid trickling down the front of his hard chest. I smear it with my hand as I move to grab hold of his muscular upper arms, fingers curling over the beautiful ink etched into his skin.

There's a dragon on one side, and several lines of kanji on the other. But that's not the most remarkable part of Weston in that moment. Instead, I can feel several piercings rubbing all the right places inside of me, bits of metal enhancing the wide, thick warmth of his cock.

Once again, I forgot to have an adult conversation

before foregoing a condom.

Shit, whatever, I like to live dangerously. And my life ... I don't expect to keep living it for much longer. Maybe I'm not at all sure that I want to? No, I'll take pleasure wherever I can get it.

"You're pierced," I whisper as I push even further down the length of him. "In multiple spots," I add with a small, choking laugh. The squeezing of my inner muscles makes West grunt as he reaches down to my hand and puts my fingers back on his wound. Apparently, I'm still holding the needle.

"Do it," he coughs, "while I'm still riding the high of being inside of you."

I swallow hard and take another look at the GSW, my head spinning from the pleasure of being stretched taut, filled, fucked. I should stitch this wound up as fast as I can, so I can ride Weston ... or see if he's feeling okay enough to flip me over and ride me.

Before I can question my own mettle, I shove the needle into his skin and his breath hisses out in a rush. I aim to make tight, narrow stitches, sealing the flesh back together without getting too close to the edges. I don't want them to tear out down the road. As I work, West clenches and unclenches his hands on my hips, his breathing ragged and broken, rife with pain.

As I do my work, he grabs a bottle of booze from the side table and takes a long, hearty sip, passing it to me. I take it in my right hand and drink my fair share, totally loving this moment. There's the metallic copper scent of blood, the fiery burn of the whiskey, and the thick heat of Weston's shaft. It's a blur of strangely beautiful sensations, made so real and crisp by the lack of drugs in my system. Where I'm at in my life, a little bit of booze isn't going to do shit but calm my nerves.

"There," I say, tying off the thread and setting the needle aside. "All done."

"Fuck, that's tight," West says, giving me a sly look that says he's not just talking about the stitches. "So much better than if Mace did it. Hurt less, quicker, and I might not even have a scar."

"So, I deserve a reward then?" I ask, sweeping his hair off his sweaty forehead. He looks tired, but okay, not like he's about to keel over anytime soon. Good thing that, since he's buried deep inside of me. I rock my hips experimentally and West groans, bucking up and slamming our pelvises together.

"You're the one who's supposed to be nursing *me* back to health?" West whispers, his voice low and thick with sex. "How about you take care of me now and as soon as I'm feeling up to it, I'll come and show you what I can do?" He reaches up and takes a handful of my brunette hair and the fabric of my habit, wrapping it around his fist and making me yelp as he jerks me toward him and takes my mouth, his piercings bumping my lip as he thrusts his tongue between them.

I can't help the sounds that escape me, these wild

noises of abandon that pour out like a symphonic sound of sin, tainting the walls of the church. I'm not a quiet girl, never have been, and I wonder if any of these noises are leaking out into the hall, teasing the other boys, or drifting through the walls and tainting the ears of poor old church ladies.

If only they were as lucky as me.

I move my hips hard and fast, grinding down against Weston's thick, hard cock. I can feel at least three piercings—one at the tip, and two along the length of his shaft. It's like having a few extra fingers down there, teasing all my best parts.

West lifts his left hand and cups my breast through the nun's habit, pulling his lips from my mouth to kiss the side of my neck. He licks my throbbing pulse, encouraging me to work harder and faster, grind our slick hungry bodies together towards orgasm.

We both pause though when the door opens, and Colt slips into the room, locking it behind him.

"I give up, bro," he says, his eyes twinkling as he takes the two of us in with a look of hunger that has my cunt clamping down and squeezing Weston with every ounce of power I have. The constriction of my muscles makes Weston curse as he spears his friend with a violent glare. "You guys are making all these sounds ..."

"Nobody invited you," West snaps, but he doesn't say anything as Colt frees his dick and wraps his hand around the base, working himself with a few sure strokes before he comes over and crawls onto the bed behind me.

My pulse is working overtime, making me dizzy as he drags my hair over my shoulder, those few loose strands that've escaped the nun's habit tickling my flesh. I think he's waiting to see if I'll tell him *no* or ask him to leave.

I don't.

Instead, I gasp as Colt takes two handfuls of the scratchy old cloth and tears it over my head, chucking it side. He scoots closer to me and teases my back with his shaft.

"Weston's too sick to properly take care of you: let me help." Colt scoots in closer and starts kissing all the places that West just took care of. Goose bumps break out across my skin. There's nothing so delicious as feeling one man kiss the spot another just vacated. They each have their own style, their own feel, and my body loves the contrast.

"You son of a bitch," West sighs, but he's clearly given up. That, and he must *feel* how excited I am as my muscles tighten, and I rock back and forth on his dick, my palms rubbing over the hard points of his nipples.

"Where do you want me?" Colt asks, putting his lips to my ear and making me shiver.

"What do you mean?" I ask, and the low sound of his chuckle makes me clench again.

"Shit, dude, you're going to make me come if you

keep fucking with her like that," West snaps at his friend. They must be super close if they're willing to share a girl like this. Based on their interaction, I doubt it's the first time.

"I *mean*," Colt continues, licking the shell of my ear. "Do you want me in the back ... or the *front*?"

"Weston's already in the front," I start, but I'm intrigued. Colt seems to know what he's doing so ... what the hell? "Can you really get it in there?" He just laughs at me, standing up off the bed and making his way over to the other side of the room. There's a second bed in here, like maybe the two men share. He opens a drawer on the nightstand and withdraws a bottle of lube, slicking up his dick with several strokes before he takes his place behind me.

The old mattress shifts as Colt pushes me forward with a single palm on my back, smashing my now bare (and still aching) breasts against Weston's hot, sweaty chest. Colt maneuvers behind me, pushing the head of his shaft up against my opening, alongside Weston's dick. At first, it doesn't feel like this is going to work, like the man is crazy, but as he pushes forward, I get this wild tight feeling and then ... he slips the rest of the way in.

The pleasure is so intense that I end up biting West's other shoulder, just about the same spot where the GSW is. Oh well. At least he can match on both sides, right?

All three of us moan as Colt starts to move,

slicking his shaft along Weston's and rubbing against my fully stretched cunt. It's so intense that I know I'm not going to last long. Luckily, I don't think either of the guys is either. This isn't a position that's meant to go on forever.

I shift and adjust myself so that my clit starts to rub with each of Colt's thrusts, making heat pool in my lower belly. My nipples pebble so tightly that they start to hurt, and my breathing devolves into these rapid, gasping breaths.

Weston comes first, clamping down so tight on my hips that I'll definitely have bruises in the morning. He throws his head back and explodes inside of me, but Colt doesn't stop moving. If anything, his friend's orgasm makes him move faster, fuck harder.

I kiss and lick and suck on Weston's sweaty skin as an outlet for all that pleasure, my own climax sneaking up on me and taking over before Colt can even finish. My body feels like it's melting from the rush of hormones, happy-go-lucky pheromones flooding my brain as I collapse and Colt comes right after, grunting as he blows his load and then pulls away, collapsing onto the bed behind me.

"First time you've ever done that, Tzarina?" he asks after a few moments, right as I'm standing up and snatching my robes from the floor. I'm not quite sure what to say to him—he's right, by the way—but I'm in need of a shower and a moment to myself. Weston looks better—much, *much* better—so I feel like I can have a moment to think.

"I …" I start, but then I'm fleeing the room, and I don't know why.

There's something inside of me that aches, something beyond the physical. I want what these guys have, their teamwork and friendship and camaraderie.

I want to belong.

I want to be their new Portia.

12

NATALIA

The next morning, I'm woken up way too goddamn early by Hawke. He's standing over my bed dressed all in black and looking like a total badass. As soon as I see him, I wish I were naked under the covers, so I could invite him to climb in with me.

Christ, Natalia, is it any surprise why you thought you might benefit from becoming a nun? I know I have problems, so sue me.

"What's going on?" I ask as Hawke chucks a stack of clothes onto the end of my bed.

"Get dressed, get up, and I'll meet you downstairs." He turns and stalks away as my mouth gapes open, and I pick through the items he left me.

New black sports bra—surprisingly one that looks like it might fit—plus a pair of black cotton panties, black sweats, and a black tank top. Underneath it all, there's a thick pair of socks and some black combat boots.

Uh-oh.

I get the feeling I'm going to get my ass kicked today.

Standing up, I take the clothes with me and sneak into the bathroom across the hall. After a quick shower, I pull my still wet hair up into a ponytail and descend into the kitchen area fully dressed and feeling kind of cool. Like Lara Croft or some shit. Although I'd prefer to have skintight shorts like her instead of these baggy sweats.

Arsen is cooking which is just *weird* now that I know him a little better. Doesn't seem right that a man that fucked-up can make such beautiful scents in the tiny kitchen. Looks like we're having sausage, hash browns, and eggs.

Hot damn.

I sit down at the table and smile when Mace supplies me with both a cup of orange juice with a single ice cube, and a steaming mug of black coffee.

"Thanks, Macey," I whisper, but it's not quiet enough. Arsen snorts a laugh and shakes his head as he continues cooking.

"Welcome," Mace replies with a gruff voice, taking the seat beside me. "We might need to come up with a new nickname though."

A teasing grin curls my lips. "Why? I like 'Macey',

it's cute."

"It makes me sound like a department store," he grumbles, and I laugh abruptly, choking on the sip of juice I'd just taken.

When I stop coughing, I wipe tears from my eyes and grin at the huge man. He's frowning at me in concern, and my heart contracts. He's *such* a nice guy ... I definitely need his dick in me soon. I bet it's massive, too. *Jesus, I'm fucked-up.*

"Alright, I'll come up with something else," I concede, just as Arsen sets a loaded plate down on the table in front of me. "Uh, is this ... for everyone?" I ask him, eyeing up the mountain of food with suspicion.

"No." He frowns down at me, still wielding a spatula in one hand. Now that he's facing me, I can see he's wearing an apron with kittens all over it. "It's for you. Eat it all, you'll need your strength for training with Hawke today."

Arsen stands there awkwardly for a moment, then hesitantly leans down and *kisses me on the forehead.* What in the actual fuck?!

He seems confused by his own actions, wrinkling his nose and spinning back to the stove to continue plating up breakfast, so I give Mace a bewildered look. Mace, though, looks just as confused as I feel and simply shakes his head at me. The message is clear: just let it go. Don't provoke the crazy man.

Shaking the odd moment off, I take a forkful of

food and chew it before speaking again. "Where is Hawke, anyway? He told me to meet him downstairs?"

"Setting up a training space," Mace replies, jerking his head in the direction of the church. "He'll be expecting you in there soon, so you'd better eat quick."

"Wait, we're training *in* the church? What if some little old lady comes in to light a prayer candle or something?" I ask, and Mace arches a brow at me. "I don't know. Isn't that what people do in churches?"

"He's locked the door and put a sign out to say we're doing repairs for a couple of days. It's just safer, especially with you being here and all." Mace nods to my food. "Eat up. I want to help out before I need to go out." He glances at his watch and grunts. "Which is in less than an hour, so chop chop, Talia."

"You ... closed the church so you could train me?" I repeat, forking another load of food into my mouth and chewing quickly. "That seems extreme."

Arsen barks another laugh at this, spinning around to face me so fast that egg goes flying off his spatula and hits the wall. "Extreme? Has no one really explained our mission to you, Miss Petrova? We're here to take down your Daddy's whole operation, sunshine. And then, once there are no commanders in place to take over, we will kill Daddy Petrov himself." He drags the spatula across his throat, as though it's a knife. "So, nothing is too *extreme* when it comes to corrupting his little princess. Is there, now?"

"You mean ... training. Right?" I hesitate, unsure of his meaning. "Because I'm fine to train, but I won't become involved in my Papa's business. Not now, not ever."

Arsen gives me a totally unhinged smile. "We'll see about that, little princess."

I open my mouth to argue, but Mace stops me with a huge hand on my wrist. "Eat, Talia. Ignore him."

Grumbling, I do as I'm told because I really am hungry and for all his insanity, Arsen knows what he's doing in the kitchen. That, and I have a bad feeling about why I would "need my strength" for whatever Hawke has planned.

Quickly, I finish two thirds of my plate before groaning and pushing it away. My appetite is better than it's been the last few days, but not even the healthiest version of me could finish all of that food.

Mace pushes back his chair and holds out a hand to me, which I take.

"Catch you later, Arsen," Mace mutters as he leads me out of the kitchen. I can't help myself: I glance over my shoulder and find Arsen's cruel, blue eyes locked on me with a stare so intense I physically shiver. He's up to something ... and my stomach is in knots with anticipation wondering what it might be.

"About time," Hawke snaps, breaking my line of thought as Mace and I enter the church. "Have you eaten sufficiently?"

The question was for me, but it's Mace who replies.

"She ate. Not enough, but better than before."

"I can speak for myself, you know," I sulk, snatching my hand back from Mace's grip and folding my arms. I despise being treated like a child.

Hawke spears me with a predatory glare. "Good. Get on the mat."

Craning my neck past the two huge men, I see seven or eight pews have been cleared from the front of the church and thin blue training mats have been laid down. The other thing that catches my eye, though, is the web of ropes draped over the altar, which has been cleared of stuff.

"What's that for?" I ask, my belly fluttering with nervous excitement.

"For stretching," Hawke tells me, but his eyes flicker with mischief. "I want to do some hand-to-hand work with you first. So get on the mat, Natalia."

"Yes, sir," I mutter sarcastically, brushing between the two men and strutting over to the middle of the blue mats. Once again, with both Hawke and Mace eyeing me like a prime rib or something, I wish I was in hot pants rather than sweats. Fucking sweats. So damn un-sexy.

"Alright, Natalia." Hawke nods, sauntering over to join me on the mat, while Mace perches on the edge of the rope-covered altar to watch. "Have you ever learned to fight before? You handled yourself pretty well in the parking lot yesterday."

"Uh, no." I shake my head, the memory of

yesterday's attack taking the wind from my sails. "Papa taught me to shoot, but that was about it."

Hawke nods again, thoughtfully. "Okay, let's see what we're working with then." He steps closer to me. "Punch me."

"Uh ..." I raise an eyebrow at him and take a nervous step back. "You want me to ..."

"Punch me. If you can." Hawke's words hold such challenge that my fists automatically curl. Did he seriously just imply I'm not *capable* of hitting him?

"Fine." I hold my ground and raise my chin stubbornly. "Anywhere in particular?"

"Lady's choice," he mocks me, and my eyes narrow. He's doing it on purpose to get a rise out of me; I know this logically. But damn him, it's working.

"Fine," I say again, tightening my fist and then whipping it out without warning to slam into Hawke's midsection. It's like hitting a fucking brick wall, and I scream in pain. "What the fuck?" I yell at him, clutching my hand to my chest and trying to bite back tears.

"I see we have a lot of work to do," Hawke sighs, stepping closer and taking my aching hand in his to inspect. "You'll be fine. At least you kept your thumb on the outside."

Scowling, I yank my hand away from him. "I'm not a total idiot."

"No, just dumb enough to hit me in the *least* vulnerable part of my body. You hit like a little girl, too. We need to work on that." Hawke purses his lips, looking down on me. "This is going to be a long day."

"Why do I even need to know this?" I demand like a petulant child. "I can shoot. Surely that's enough to keep me alive for a few days?"

Hawke walks away from me, towards some equipment beside the mat, but when I say this, he pauses and looks back at me. "A few days?" he repeats. "What happens after that?"

I shrug. I hadn't really meant to say that out loud, but it's been a tiring few days. "I'll be dead. That's what. You can't think Dmitri and the others would be the only attempt Papa will make to take me back?"

"And ... you think he'll kill you?" Hawke queries me, his eyes narrowed.

A humorless, bitter sounding laugh chuckles out of me. "Unfortunately, I don't. Not for a long, *long* time, anyway. That's why I'll kill myself before I let him get to me."

Hawke simply stares at me for a long, tense moment, then gives a short nod and turns away to pick up some punching pads. "I see. Well, then we best get started."

He returns to me, his face closed-off and cold, holding out a pair of gloves which I strap on without another word. I have a feeling he's the kind of guy who'd try to talk me out of suicide, so his lack of response is ... confusing.

"Let's begin," Hawke instructs me. "Hit the pads

one after another until I say stop."

Biting the inside of my lip to keep my trap shut, I nod my understanding and move as he tells me to. For what feels like hours, we continue like this. Me doing what Hawke says, and him correcting little things as we go. My stance, the angle of my elbow, the shift of my hips as I throw a punch ... the whole thing is utterly exhausting, but even I have to admit I'm making improvements.

Hawke *seems* to agree, but getting compliments out of him is like squeezing blood from a stone, I'm learning. Whether he does or not, he eventually calls an end to the drills he has me running, and I collapse into a boneless heap on the mat.

"Get up, Natalia," he orders me sharply, tossing his pads aside and strapping on gloves of his own. "No rest. You need to put these new skills into practical use."

"What do you mean?" I groan, reluctantly rolling to my feet. I get my answer when Hawke throws a punch at my face which I just barely manage to dodge in time to avoid a broken nose.

"What the fuck, Hawke?" I yell. "That's fighting dirty! I wasn't ready!"

"Natalia, sweets. We're for-hire mercenaries and assassins. Not the fucking NYPD. All we *do* is fight dirty." Hawke gives me a grim smile, bouncing lightly on his toes as I circle away from him. "Besides, you need to learn what it feels like to be hit. If you know what to expect, you'll hesitate less in battle. You won't lock-up with fright. Knowledge of pain might save your life one day."

"So what?" I rage. "I'm supposed to just let you punch me?"

"No," he smirks. "You're supposed to fight back. If you can."

My eyes narrow, and I curl my lip in anger. Hawke doesn't leave time for me to reply as he darts in close and throws another punch at me, this time aimed at my midsection. I dodge and stumble, but his knuckles still glance off my ribs.

I cry out with pain. He sure as shit isn't fucking around, and as much as my ribs are hurting, it could've been a whole lot worse if he'd landed the full force on me. He was right though, for a second there when his knuckles connected, and white-hot pain flared, I froze.

"Come on, Natalia," he taunts me. "You can hit back if you want. It'll make you feel better about the beating you're going to take from me."

Sweat drips down my spine, and I lock my jaw, refusing to be baited. It's what he wants, for me to lose control and forget everything he's been teaching me all day. I watch enough action movies to know how these things roll.

I will take him up on the offer to hit back, though. Using my smaller size, I duck under a lazy fist he throws in my direction and jab a sharp punch into his

ALTERED BY FIRE

side. I'm banking on the fact that he might have somewhat less muscle coverage at the side, but I'm thwarted when it feels like I'm hitting rock.

Hawke chuckles and returns the favor with a hit to my gut which I have no hope of dodging. His closed fist meets my weak abdominal muscles and the air rushes out of me as I fall to the floor.

"Get up, Natalia," Hawke orders, but there's a trace of mocking in his voice. "I didn't even hit you that hard. Come on."

I'm incapable of words as I clutch my belly and try to find my breath again, but I'm nothing if not a stubborn bitch, so I push back to my feet and glare at Hawke. My *trainer*. Call me crazy, but when the guys had said Hawke would be training me today, I'd sort of thought he'd be training me in *something else*. Something requiring a whole lot less clothing and hopefully the inclusion of those ropes on the altar.

I heave a sigh. Yeah, pretty sure I was wrong on that front. These bastards really do mean to train me in how to *fight*.

Hawke and I circle each other, trading a few more blows for a while until my whole body feels black and blue. Hawke's strike rate compared to mine is laughable, but that's sort of the point, isn't it?

"Okay, I'm done," I declare, collapsing onto the mat. My breath is coming in short, sharp gasps and I'm drenched in sweat. Not to mention the fact that my body feels like it's been shoved in a barrel and tossed over Niagara Falls. *Everything* hurts.

"We're not done yet," Hawke tells me and I groan. He's standing over me and unstrapping his gloves. The fucker isn't even sweating! "Hop up, it's time to stretch out your muscles or you'll lock up tomorrow." I let out a dramatic sob, but take his hand when he offers it to me, pulling me up from the mat.

"You'll need to remove your sweats," Hawke continues, leading me over to the altar which this morning I'd seriously thought was set for some kinky bondage sex play. Now, though, I'm pretty sure it's as boring as Hawke said. Stretching. "I need to be able to see your muscles."

Fighting a smile, because I'm a dirty bitch who's still thinking about sex, I drop my sweatpants and strip my shirt off. This leaves me in just my panties and sports bra, and I hear a low whistle from the choir balcony.

"Don't mind me," Arsen snickers, perched on the edge of the railing. "Just came to watch."

Hawke flicks a glance up to him and grunts a noise in his throat. "Ignore him. I do. Come on, hop up." He taps the flat top of the altar with the palm of his hand, and I climb up as gracefully as I can manage.

"Uh, isn't this a little bit sacrilegious?" I tease, laying down on my back the way Hawke indicates.

"What? Using the church altar to *stretch* you out?" Hawke puts an odd emphasis on that word that has my mind straight back in the gutter. "Considering Arsen is sitting up there in the choir balcony wearing his priestly robes while smoking a cigarette, this isn't near as bad, right?"

I smile, remembering the *sacrilegious* things I did with Colt only a few nights ago. "You're right. Proceed, oh great combat master. Give me your worst."

"Careful what you wish for, Natalia," he chuckles, moving around the altar to take one of my wrists. He extends my arm away from my body and secures it with the rope attached to the top corner. The cord is soft, silken, and I suspect it's been borrowed from somewhere else within the church. Too bad Mace left hours ago. I'm already missing him, and I'd like to see his reaction to this, see if his eyes might sparkle with lust, or his pants tent in excitement.

"What's that supposed to mean?" I ask, a little breathlessly as he takes my other wrist and does the same to that side. The angles tug a little at my muscles, but it's basically just like an intense pilates workout so far.

Hawke gives me a little smirk, but doesn't respond as he moves around to my feet and then climbs up onto the flat surface with me and grasps one of my ankles. He locks eyes with me as he lifts my leg up high, straightening my knee and pushing my leg closer and closer to my face.

Silly Hawke must not have done his homework on the mob princess, though, as he looks impressed with the range of flexibility in my leg.

"Keep going," I tell him when my ankle is mere inches from my face. "Fifteen years of ballet and gymnastics, I can take it harder."

His eyes flare with interest and he pushes me further until my foot touches the altar beside my head. He holds it there for a long moment, his body pressing down on top of me and his gaze locked on mine. This is exciting him, I can tell by the hard bulge pressing against my crotch, and I let out a small sigh of arousal.

"This was a bad idea," he mutters, releasing my leg and swapping for the other one. "All I want to do is tie you down, spread you wide open right here, and sink my dick inside you."

"So?" I gasp as he presses my other leg up in a stretch. "Do it."

Hawke's eyes narrow as his weight bears down on me and his hard cock brushes against my throbbing center again. "You actually mean that, don't you?" he murmurs with curiosity. "You actually want me to tie you down and fuck you here on this church altar."

His words alone send a heady rush of excitement through me, and I moan. "Fuck yes. Don't make me beg for it, Hawke."

He sucks in a deep breath, releasing my leg and kneeling between my spread thighs. "You are awfully hard to say no to, Natalia ..." he ponders aloud, stroking his thumbs under the waistband of my black cotton panties. Thankfully, he must be just as turned-on as I am right now, because he drags the damp fabric down my legs and tosses them aside.

Amusingly, from the corner of my eye, I see them hit a carved wooden statue of an angel and hang over her face like a blindfold. I don't waste time laughing at it though, as Hawke grasps my ankle in his firm grip and winds rope around it.

"Maybe I should have made you beg," he mutters as he works, looping the cord over and over around my skin, bending my leg and linking my ankle to the back of my thigh. He then proceeds to tie me directly to the altar itself. Suffice to say that by the time he's finished replicating this on the other side, I'm not only spread wide open and so secure I can barely move an inch, I'm also soaking wet with arousal.

"Wait," I pant as he tosses his shirt off and goes for his pants. "Will you wear the robe?"

Hawke pauses, looking down at me with an eyebrow raised. "Seriously?" He sighs, and closes his eyes for a moment. When he opens them back up, they're burning with lustful shadows. "Well, I don't see why not. Wait here." He chuckles and disappears from view, presumably to fetch his priestly robe. Fuck me, just the idea of being pounded by Hawke's thick cock while he's in disguise almost has me coming right here without stimulation.

I lie there for what feels like ages, spread open with my pussy aimed right up at the stained-glass angels of the windows. They smile down on me, serene, and I think even a little mischievous ... We've all heard stories of angels corrupting human women, so I like to think those bastards would enjoy this show.

Hawke's footsteps announce his arrival before he climbs back up onto the altar to kneel between my outstretched and bound thighs. He's done exactly as I asked, and thrown on his billowy black robe and even included the little white collar. Below the collar, he's left the robe open and I can see the chiseled expanse of his body, covered in swirling ink all the way down. *All* the way down. The only part of his body from neck to knee that isn't illustrated is his big beautiful penis which stands proudly out of the cloth as though straining to be inside me.

"Fuck," I breathe, taking him in with wide eyes. "I missed out on this view last time."

"Natalia," he snaps, arching a brow at me. "No more talking. Or do I need to gag you?"

Licking my lips, I shake my head. "No, Father."

This seems to tip his control, and he launches at me, grasping my rope covered thighs and thrusting his tip just inside me before swearing and pulling back.

"What—" I start to say, then remember the *no talking* rule. Hawke growls a noise, digging in one of the deep pockets of his robe and pulling out a condom. With savage efficiency he tears it free from the packet and rolls it down his length, smoothing his hand a few times along his shaft once it's on.

It's a bit twisted of me, given *none* of us have engaged in the safe-sex talk, but I kind of wish he'd ride me bareback. There's just something ... *extra* about it. Maybe it's the danger? The unknown risk? Especially when they come inside me like Arsen, Weston, and Colt had. Then again, it's all just an illusion of risk when likely, I'll be dead by month's end. No time to develop any pesky diseases or pregnancies.

Hawke's oblivious to my sinful thoughts though, as he returns his tip to my opening and pushes inside ever so slowly.

I groan at the exquisite torture of it, as he slides into me bit by bit. I want to beg, scream, cry out for more. But Hawke has a mean streak, and I just know he'd do the opposite, so I bite my lip and moan as he fills me with his dick.

Eventually, he's in and my cunt clenches around him, hugging him tight, making him groan.

"Jesus Christ, Natalia. Your pussy is like a clamp; it makes me want to blow my load right now." He withdraws halfway and pumps back in with absolutely zero urgency. It's utterly maddening, and I'm panting so hard I'm starting to see stars. "Good thing I'm no amateur." He gives me a wicked grin and adjusts his position so that he's sort of kneeling, his legs spread wide for balance and his cock still firmly entrenched inside me.

He reaches out and palms my tits in his hands,

rolling my nipples between his fingers as he continues his lazy pace with small thrusts of his hips. Bound as I am, I'm totally helpless to make him move faster, to give me what I want. And that's exactly what *he* wants ...

"You're dying to say something; I can see it all over your face," he comments, pinching my nipples sharply and making me cry out. "I'm impressed that you haven't cracked yet. Maybe you really can be trained." His fingers pinch my nipples again, but I'm expecting it this time and just moan into the sensation.

A noise from somewhere else in the church makes me gasp, and I look askance at Hawke, who frowns in the direction of the noise, over my head. When he sees who it is, he simply rolls his eyes and continues thrusting into me.

Just as I open my mouth to ask what's going on, I get my answer with the smell of cigarettes and bourbon as Arsen licks the side of my face.

"Arsen," I moan, feeling my pussy tighten with excitement that he's come to join us. He'd been so silent since Hawke began tying me down, I really had forgotten he was there.

"Natalia," Hawke sighs, gripping my waist tight enough to bruise, "What did I tell you about speaking?"

I mew a small, half-hearted protest, but it's Arsen who responds. "Don't stress it boss, I'll take care of this naughty mouth." He meets my gaze, upside down as he leans over me from above, and his own ice-blue eyes flickering with insanity. I have a solid idea of what he means by that, and I can't fucking wait.

My tongue darts out of my mouth and drags over my lips suggestively as Arsen's hand caresses my throat.

"Fine," Hawke grunts, "but hurry the hell up. We're expecting a visit from Sister Frances later, and I still need to clear all of this up."

"Yes, sir," Arsen mocks, hauling himself up onto the altar above my head and tossing his robes back dramatically. He's already freed his cock from his black slacks, and he slaps it against my cheek as he positions himself. "Open up, Miss Petrova. I wanna see you suck my cock just as good as you did Colt's in the confessional."

Awash with excitement and arousal, I open my lips as commanded and Arsen roughly jams his dick down my throat without ceremony. For a moment, I choke and panic, but my years of experience reign supreme as my throat relaxes, and I suck air through my nose.

"Fuck yeah, bitch. Just like that," Arsen growls, fucking my mouth as I do my best to suck and lick at his shaft. Without hands, I can only do so much, but the helplessness seems to be half the turn on here.

Hawke, too, increases his pace, pounding into my pussy like he has something to prove. It's a shame I can't see him, what with Arsen straddling my face, but just knowing the two of them are screwing me with their collars and robes on is sending me into a spiral that I just know will result in multiple orgasms.

From the way my head is tilted, all I can see—other than Arsen's balls—is the side door to the church and the wooden cross hanging over it.

Gagged as I am with Arsen's cock, all I can do is moan as these two dirty fake priests take me hard and fast. Hawke's fingers dance across my clit, flicking and pinching at my ultra-charged nerve endings, and I release a muffled scream along with my first orgasm.

There's more to come, though; I can feel them building like a set of waves and the third is always the biggest.

Just as I think I'm about to skip into my second, Hawke withdraws from me completely. I cry out a protest around Arsen's dick, trying to wiggle my tightly bound hips in encouragement, but I barely move an inch.

"Shh," Arsen purrs, stroking the column of my neck. "Hawke's just getting an extra little treat for you. Now keep sucking, you have a mouth like a fucking Hoover, and I'm just dying to come down your throat."

An extra little treat? I'm not left wondering for long, as something cold and hard is stroked down the length of my cunt and then dipped inside. It's not quite as thick as Hawke's cock, but it's long and Hawke pumps it in and out of me a few times before dragging it down to my asshole.

"Fuck yeah," Arsen encourages as his fingers grip my throat.

Hawke responds by pressing the object against my tight hole, breaching the ring of muscle slowly and making me cry out with ecstasy. Whatever he's using, it's been thoroughly lubed with my own juices so offers little resistance as he pushes it further inside me.

"Perfect," Hawke breathes when he's inserted the round object as far as he wants. "How's that, Natalia?"

I moan my muffled approval, and Arsen chuckles a dark sound.

"I'd say she fucking loves it," Arsen replies for me, withdrawing his cock from my mouth and slapping it across my face. "What do you think, Miss Petrova?" He allows me enough space to raise my head just an inch, to look down between my legs.

"Holy shit," I breathe, seeing the white tip of a candle protruding from my ass. "Fuck yes."

Both men laugh and Arsen gives me no further respite before holding my jaw open and shoving his rock-hard erection back into my mouth. I feel Hawke shift, his hot cock pressing back inside me, only this time it's with the extra stretch of having my asshole filled at the same time.

When Hawke bottoms out, filling my pussy just as the candle is filling my ass, I scream into my next orgasm. I've mentioned before that I'm one of those lucky bitches who can orgasm on vaginal penetration only, but this is just next level.

Hawke grunts curses as he pounds into me, and I know he's close. Arsen, too, as I can see his balls tightening and feel his shaft beginning to pulse against my tongue. I need to come one more time, but have a feeling that won't be *any* issue the way this is going.

"Use your teeth," Arsen orders me, and I oblige, scraping my teeth along his length as he pumps into my mouth. He's insane, so I know he gets off on the danger, and I press harder than I usually would, which seems to work for him. "Shit yeah," he grunts, his hand tightening around my neck.

He starts coming as his hand tightens even further, and my vision starts to go black from lack of oxygen. I don't want him to stop though, not for a fucking second. He pulls out of my mouth abruptly, coming on my tongue instead of the back of my throat where I can't taste it, and I swallow.

"Fuck," Hawke swears as I put on a show of licking Arsen's slick tip, and then Hawke's coming, too. As he finishes, he abruptly yanks the candle back out of my ass, and I spiral into my third orgasm, *screaming* as my body convulses and shivers through the overwhelming sensations.

As my cries fade, the sound of something hitting the floor jolts us from the post-sex haze.

"Shit!" Hawke yells, leaping off me while Arsen begins cackling with laughter.

"What is it?" I demand, but Arsen just seals his lips

to mine, kissing me deeply before releasing my face.

"That was fun. Let's do it again, sometime." Without any further explanation, he hops off the altar and saunters away, whistling like a fruit loop.

Unobstructed by his body, I can turn my head just enough to see Hawke crouched over someone in the aisle of the church and doing what seems like ... chest compressions?

"Hawke! What the fuck is going on? Who is that?" I demand, thrashing against my bonds but getting nowhere. Hawke seriously knew what he was doing when he tied me down.

"Fuck, where the fuck did Arsen just go?" he bellows back at me, looking panicked.

"How the fuck do I know? I'm a little tied down here!" I scream back at him, freaking out because *he's* freaking out. "Who is that?"

"Fucking fuck!" Hawke curses. "It's Sister Frances. I think she just had a heart attack when she saw us ... you know ..."

"Oh for the love of God," I exclaim, and the irony is not lost on me. "Untie me, so I can get help!"

"I can't," he pants. "I have to keep up compressions."

I groan, and tug on my restraints again. This is *not* cool. For several minutes I just lie there on my back, my legs spread and the result of my own orgasms slick on my cunt, until thankfully someone else shows up.

"What ... the shit have you been up to in here?"

Weston grins, entering from the doorway that leads to the living quarters. He's dressed casually in sweats and a T-shirt, with his arm in a sling to protect his gunshot wound.

"West," I exclaim. "Thank fuck! Can you untie me, please?"

The tall, Asian man stands beside the altar for a while, running his eyes over me like he's considering *not* letting me go, before tugging on a few cords and magically freeing me.

"Thank you," I sigh, unwrapping the silken cord from my limbs and shaking out some stiffness.

"What happened to the old broad?" he asks, jerking his head toward Hawke who's still counting out compressions on the woman's chest.

"Uh, I think she walked in while Hawke and Arsen were fucking me in their priest robes," I admit, not even the slightest bit uncomfortable. It was fucking epic sex, nothing to be ashamed of there!

"She had a heart attack," Hawke informs us, grunting as he keeps his rhythm.

I frown. "Shouldn't we call an ambulance?"

"Can't." Weston shakes his head and passes me my panties from off the angel's head. "It'd risk blowing our cover. Besides, I'm pretty sure she's a goner, Hawke."

Hawke sighs, sitting back and mopping sweat from his forehead with his robes. "Yeah, I'm pretty sure she is, too. Alright, go grab Colt for me. We'll need to set her up to look like this happened in her own home."

"You got it, boss," Weston replies with a little mock salute before disappearing back the way he came.

"What do you need me to do?" I ask, sliding off the edge of the altar and dragging my sweatpants on. "Carry her bible or something?" I nudge the heavy book with my toe and realize that was the sound we'd heard at the end of my climax. The old nun must have dropped the book in shock.

"You don't seem in the least bit concerned about the presence of a dead woman," Hawke observes me with narrowed eyes. "Have you really seen so much death in your life that this doesn't affect you?"

I give a shrug. "Pretty much. So how can I help?"

Hawke sighs again. "Just go up to your room and take it easy. You'll be pretty sore from that training session today, and I expect you'll have one or two bruises coming up."

"I'm sure I will," I agree with a saucy sounding murmur. Hawke has his no-nonsense voice on, though, so I do as he tells me and head out of the church and up the stairs to my little room.

Once my door is closed, I strip out of my sweaty clothes and stand naked in front of the mirror. Hawke was right: my body's already showing the shadows of multiple bruises from his fists, but the ones that make me smile are smaller. Fingerprint sized. On my thighs, my waist, my breasts, and darkest of all ... around my neck.

I shiver as I remember the feeling of the ropes binding me, of Arsen's hand around my throat and Hawke's pinning my thighs. I'm playing with fire, and I fucking love it.

13

COLT

I'm laughing so hard I have to dab at my eyes with the sleeve of my sweatshirt before looking back over at Hawke.

"You're kidding me," I say again, still not totally believing what I'm hearing.

"I wish I was," Hawke murmurs, drumming his fingers on the steering wheel, "Right as Natalia is coming for the third time, Sister Francis has a heart attack. If she hadn't dropped that huge fucking bible, we probably wouldn't have noticed, Natalia was screaming so loud."

I burst out in another peal of laughter. It's too damn funny. I mean, shit about the nun dying—that's never ideal—but seriously ... how long had she been standing there watching?

"So much for locking the door, huh boss?" Mace snickers from the backseat where he's strapped in beside Sister Frances' corpse.

Hawke growls. "I *did* lock the fucking door. Turns out, she had a key."

We all snicker at this one. What are the odds? That poor old woman would have had the fright of her life watching two "priests" fucking the stuffing out of a naked girl tied to the altar.

"Was it worth it though?" Mace asks with a faraway look on his face that makes me double take.

Hawke must see him in the mirror too, because he jerks a quick look at Mace over his shoulder. "You can't tell me you haven't ..."

"Sure you have." I frown, turning in my seat to look at the big man. "You had that trip to the gun range, and we all know how hot it is to see a chick that can shoot. You want to tell us you didn't nail her in the Hummer?"

Mace gives me a weird look. Like he's constipated or something, but I'm not getting it.

"Mace?" Hawke prompts and the big man gusts out a heavy sigh.

"No, I didn't. Talia ... she's different. She's not like Portia. I kind of like her, you know?" Mace is clearly not thinking about what he's saying, and my eyes dart quickly over to Hawke whose knuckles are turning white on the steering wheel. "Not that I didn't like Portia, it's just ... Talia."

"Don't forget," Hawke snarls from between clenched teeth, "we are *using* her. We need *her* to love *us*. Not the other way around. This job has no room for real emotions, Mace. Not from us. You know that."

"I know, boss," Mace snaps back. "I'm not stupid. I just wasn't in the mood to stick my dick in her in the back of my car."

Hawke and I exchange a look. In all the years we've known Mace, he's *never* not been in the mood. This is bad. Real bad.

"Buddy, do us a favor when we get back to the church?" I say with a nervous laugh. "And get that monster cock of yours wet. I think this priest disguise is messing with your head. Making you into a *nice guy* or some shit. Trust me, a good thorough bang with that hellcat will set you straight."

Mace glares at me so hard that I turn back around in my seat. Scary ass motherfucker.

"I'll think about it," he says in a quiet, angry voice.

"You'll do it," Hawke snaps, "that's an order."

Mace grunts his understanding and a tense sort of silence falls over the three of us.

"And stop talking about fucking Portia," Hawke adds after a long pause, "She's dead, and soon enough Konstantin Petrov will follow. We don't need to keep taking trips down memory fucking lane."

"Sorry, boss," Mace mutters, and I murmur my understanding.

Hawke's hands are still clenched tight on the

steering wheel, and I keep watch from the corner of my eye. He and Arsen fell the hardest for Portia, even if they'll never admit it. Taking this job was supposed to be cathartic, *closure* for us all ... except I doubt any of us expected Natalia ... *Tzarina*.

I cover my smile with a hand, lest Hawke think I'm smiling at him.

God forbid. He'll totally kick my ass.

"This must be it," Hawke mutters, pulling into the driveway of a little cottage. "Let's get her inside and set the scene before anyone sees us."

The three of us fall into business mode. I take lookout, as usual, while Hawke picks the old bird's lock and Mace hauls her dead body inside. The aim is just to drop her somewhere inside, so it looks like she had her heart attack *here* and not in our undercover base.

We work as a well-oiled machine, and the stage is set in under five minutes. Another thirty seconds sees all traces of us erased and back on the road. We're in a stolen car, which we'll change the plates on as soon as we we're back, so there's no real danger if any of Sister Frances' neighbors saw us pull up.

"Still can't believe you killed a nun," I mutter with a cheeky grin as I glance at Hawke. "That must have been some explicit sex to give the old duck a heart attack."

Hawke shoots me a glare. "Nothing out of the ordinary. Besides, as old as she was, it was bound to happen sooner or later."

"What?" Mace snorts a laugh. "Walking in on two priests fucking a chick tied to the church altar? Yeah, that shit happens all the damn time."

"In your case, it damn well should," Hawke snaps, and the warning is clear.

Shifting to turn in my seat, I give Mace a grin. "Don't worry, bro. I have an eight ball in my room if you need a little Colombian Marching Powder to get the job done. We all know you fuck like a demon on coke."

"Colt," Hawke barks, and I slide back into my seat. He's such a stiff sometimes, considering what we do for a living. I mean fuck, he just killed a nun and he wants to give me shit for drugs? "Are you all set for this Sunday? Arsen's intel suggests Petrov is changing his routine, so he could pick our church as soon as this week."

"Yes, boss," I sigh. "All prepped and ready on my end. Are we still expecting the high-ranking members, or have they gotten cautious?"

"So far, seems to be the same pay grade doing the exchanges," Hawke confirmed.

The whole reason we're set up in the church as fake priests is because Petrov has been using the holy ground as a convenient location to make drug and money exchanges. We've known this for ages, so have the feds, but the local Bishop has refused any sort of stakeouts on church land without *proof* that they're

UNDERCOVER SINNERS

housing illegal activity.

Lucky for us, we don't give a rat's ass about rules. When we saw an opportunity open, with a new priest coming to take over Our Lady of Sorrows, we just swooped in and took his place. Not that we killed the guy; this incident with Sister Frances is a total accident. Father James is just tied up in the basement until our job is done and Petrov is dead.

Our plan, if all goes accordingly, is to identify the members of Petrov's mob and pluck them off one by one until he has no support system in place to take over. And then kill him, of course.

"He's a smart prick, I'll give him that," I mutter aloud as I stare out the window, a bit lost in my own thoughts.

"Who is?" Hawke asks.

"Petrov," I clarify. "Keeping the identities of his inner circle secret is a fucking smart move for a mobster. If we'd known who they all were, this bullshit would be over and done with by now."

"He had to know we'd work it out sooner or later," Mace rumbles from the backseat. "After what he did to Portia, he has to know this is personal now."

"Also, we have a secret weapon." The tight smile on Hawke's face sends a shiver through me. For all my teasing Mace, I actually kind of like Natalia, too ... like, for real. Not just to *gain her trust* like we're supposed to be doing. Or for a stupid bet.

"Boss, we're not doing anything to hurt her, are

we?" I ask hesitantly. I'm not totally sure I want to hear his answer when he cuts a glare at me before turning his eyes back on the road.

"We'll do with her whatever we need to, to get the job done. Understood?" His voice is cold, and I exchange a worried look with Mace in the mirror.

"Yes, boss," we both respond, but the conversation falls flat after that. Portia's death affected all of us, but it hit Hawke and Arsen the hardest. They're way more alike than they're comfortable with.

This new cruel streak Hawke is showing concerns me though. None of us are any fucking saints, but *usually* Hawke is the strongest moral voice amongst us. Now though ... well I think I'll stick a bit closer to Tzarina. Just in case.

14

NATALIA

Weston's broad shoulders shuffling around the kitchen make me sigh. He's trying to make coffee, by the looks of things, but he *should* be resting.

"Hey, West," I bark from the doorway, making him jump.

"Jesus fucking tits, Natalia," he curses, sucking spilled coffee off his fingers. "Don't sneak up on a guy like that! I could have killed you or something."

"Uh-huh, sure," I snicker. "Pretty sure the only thing you're killing is that cup of coffee. It's about to —" My warning is cut short by his elbow catching his mug on the edge of the bench and sending it crashing to the floor "—fall."

"Shit," he groans, pouting down at the mess on the tiles. "Do you have any idea how hard it is to make coffee with only one hand?" He indicates to his other arm, still strapped across his body with a sling to stop the gunshot wound reopening.

"I can imagine," I grin. "Shouldn't you be resting anyway? Why don't you head back upstairs, and I'll bring the coffee up to you? I'll clean all this up, too."

Weston hesitates, looking at the puddle of coffee and broken cup shards around his feet. "Are you sure? I feel bad, but ..." he trails off and grimaces down at his immobile arm.

"It's totally fine. After all, you *did* get shot saving my life. You have no idea what Dmitri would have done to me if you guys hadn't been there." I shudder at the morbid, blood-splattered thoughts skittering across my mind.

"Ah well," Weston gives me a sly smile, "when you put it like that, perhaps you'll deliver that coffee in that sexy fucking nun's outfit you wore the other day."

I grin back at him, even as my nipples are tightening with arousal. "We'll see. Now get upstairs, I won't be long here."

Weston does as he's told, stepping away from the mess and smacking a quick kiss on my lips as he passes me. As fucked up as this whole situation I'm in is, that little gesture of *normal* affection brings a tear to my eye and within moments I find myself sobbing silent tears as I mop up coffee from the floor.

If I'm totally honest, I don't really know *why* I'm crying. But given a good guess, it could be the fact that in my life I've never really had a "boyfriend". Not someone who gives quick kisses on his way out of the room ... or maybe I'm crying for the fact that I won't ever really get to enjoy the bonds I'm forming with these bad boys.

I'm no quitter though, so if anything they're just giving me incentive to stay out of my father's clutches as long as possible. After all, I'm not *actually* suicidal. Not in the traditional sense of the word. I just know that if push comes to shove, I'd rather take my own life than let my father exact revenge for what he'd undoubtedly see as betrayal.

Swiping the tears from my cheeks, I pull myself together and dump the broken mug into the trash. First thing, Weston needs to rest, no matter how much I want to go up there and let him bend me over to fuck me like a damn punishment.

I decide to skip the coffee because who am I kidding? I still don't know how to work that damn machine. Instead I heat up a cup of milk and make him a hot chocolate. Everyone knows hot chocolate helps you sleep, right?

Well, hot chocolate laced with crushed sleeping pills does anyway.

Carrying it up to Weston's room, I tap awkwardly

on his door. What is the etiquette here, anyway? Who knows. He calls out for me to come in anyway, so I push the door open and step through.

"Aw," he pouts when he sees me still dressed in sweatpants and a borrowed t-shirt.

I roll my eyes and bump the door closed behind me. "You need *sleep*, West. Not sex. Not *right now* anyway."

"But later?" he asks so hopefully I can't fight the grin spreading over my face.

"Later. I promise. Here, I made you hot chocolate instead of coffee." I hold the mug out to him and he accepts it with a satisfied smile.

"Come lie with me for a bit?" he suggests, shuffling over in his little single bed. "Nothing dirty, I promise. I just want to spend a bit of time with you, Natalia."

My lips pursed, I narrow my eyes at him. I *should* say no, something tells me I should. But … it's been so damn long since I just cuddled with a man. Besides, he's hot as fuck. Like, scorching. I'd be mad to say no. So instead, I cross those few steps to the bed and slide in beside him.

"Tell me if I bump your shoulder," I order him, and he grunts his agreement. He's sitting up against the pillows a little bit, sipping on his laced beverage, so I cuddle into his side and rest my cheek on his chest.

"Mm, this is nice," he murmurs after a little while, and I can hear his voice already thickening with sleep. He reaches over me and places the mug down on his bedside table. "Maybe I do need a little nap."

"Mm hmm," I agree, trying not to laugh as he wriggles down the bed and turns me over so that he's spooning me. Or ... forking me as the case is. "Weston," I groan, feeling his hard length pressed against my butt, but the only response I get is his soft snores as the sleeping pills do their job.

Well shit. I peer over my shoulder at his sleeping face. *Maybe I used too much ...*

For a few minutes, I simply lie there and watch him. But when all seems normal, and he doesn't start foaming at the mouth or anything, I relax. He must have just been really tired.

Unable to stop myself, I trail a light finger over his face, brushing a peacock green lock of hair behind his ear and then tracing over his many piercings. My breath catches, and I remember his face isn't the only place Weston is pierced.

Damn it, Natty. Pull it together, he's injured and sleeping for God's sake.

Agreeing with my chatty subconscious, I peel myself away from his warm body and slip out of the bed. On soft feet, I tiptoe out of Weston's room and carefully close the door behind me, before turning and almost screaming.

"Arsen!" I hiss, clutching a hand to my chest in an attempt to calm my racing heart. "What the fuck are you doing? You almost gave me a heart attack."

"What am *I* doing?" he repeats, stepping closer into

ALTERED BY FIRE

my personal space and boxing me against Weston's door. "What are *you* doing? Playing Florence Nightingale, are we? Pretty sure you need to be in a nun's habit for that role, Miss Petrova."

My cheeks flush with heat, and I drop my eyes away from his intense gaze. "I was just bringing him a drink. He needs rest."

Arsen grabs my chin in a bruising grip, forcing my gaze back up to meet his. For a long moment he just stares back at me, his breath harsh and a small frown creasing his forehead, like he's confused or something.

"And do you, Miss Petrova?" he whispers in a harsh tone. "Do you need ... *rest*?"

My breath catches, and I have no doubt what he's referring to, so I shake my head just the tiniest bit that his grip will allow. "No. I'm rested just fine." My own voice is drenched in sex and blatant desire. What was it about this psychopath that turns me on so hard, every damn time?

"So I see," he smirks, and his other hand snakes down the front of my sweatpants to push inside my tight pussy. His hand shifts from my chin down to my throat, and he uses it to hold me pinned to Weston's door while his fingers thrust into me a couple of times. "Well-rested."

He withdraws his hand and slowly licks his fingers. I shiver with arousal, and a small whimper escapes my throat. This seems to trigger something in him, because in a flash, he's pulled a gleaming sharp dagger and it's pressing against my throat where his fingers had rested just moments before.

"Arsen," I gasp, but he shushes me with a finger to my lips.

"I could slit your throat, you know," he tells me, like I'm not already aware of the danger. "Just one little slice, and Princess Petrova is no more. Tell me, darling, what do you think your Daddy would do if I had your pretty head delivered to him in a gift box?"

Something dark and sick inside me is responding to his threats like a damn cat in heat, and I moan softly, letting my lashes flutter.

Arsen keeps the knife to my throat, but his other hand shoves my sweats down roughly, and I kick them off my feet. "You're almost as fucked-up as me, aren't you?" he snickers as he frees his thick cock from his pants. "You want me to fuck you right here, with this knife against your throat, don't you?"

As if he needs my response. I hitch my leg up around his waist and drag him closer to me so that he can feel how turned-on I am. "Yes," I pant, feeling the cold steel against my neck and trying not to move too much, "Please, Arsen. Fuck me."

He chuckles a dark sound, and lines his cock up to my core. "Don't move, Miss Petrova. Or do ... I've never been against a little blood with my sex."

With this, he thrusts deep inside me, and I feel the blade nick my skin as I jolt with his entry. Whether it's deliberate or not, I don't give a shit. The sharp sting of the cut, followed by the drip of blood down my throat has me shuddering into a spontaneous orgasm before he's even completed one thrust.

"You sick, twisted bitch," Arsen pants, his eyes glued to the blood running down my neck while his thick cock pounds me into Weston's door. His breath is coming fast, and I know he'll be quick, so I tighten my Kegels and squeeze him with all I've got.

With a growl, he withdraws his blade from my throat and slams it into the door beside my head so hard that it probably protrudes from the other side. I don't get a second to consider it though, as Arsen dips his head low and licks a slow line up my neck, catching the falling blood and swallowing it.

Holy fucking shit. That's next level crazy, and one of the sexiest things I've ever seen.

My hand snakes between us, giving my clit the couple of quick tweaks that it needs to skyrocket me into another orgasm, and Arsen joins me. His hot load spills inside me with a few hard pumps and then ... he's gone.

By the time the stars fade from my eyes, and I pry my eyelids open, Arsen is nowhere to be seen. The only evidence that I haven't imagined the whole damn thing is the semen sliding down my thighs and the blood soaking into my t-shirt.

What the fuck was that?

I wince as I touch a hand to my neck, then bend to pull my sweats back on.

UNDERCOVER SINNERS

That was just a taste of what that psycho has to offer, and you damn well know it, Natty.

I've said it before and I'll say it again. I'm playing with fire, but I fucking love it ...

After cleaning up in the little shared bathroom, I drag the first aid kit out and patch up my neck as best I can. It's not a bad cut, but it is enough to need a bandage, so I swab on some iodine and then tape a gauze pad over the top. By the time I'm done, the bleeding has pretty much stopped; it just stings like a bitch.

Sighing to myself, I stash the medical box back where I found it and then hunt the kitchen for some booze. I'm no idiot, and am well aware that alcohol thins the blood. But like I said, it wasn't a bad cut. It certainly wouldn't kill me to have a few glasses of that Russian vodka Colt pulled out the other night.

Ah.

There it is.

I pull the bottle out of the cabinet and unscrew the top. There's a reason the Russian word for water is applied to this alcohol; it's so damn easy to drink. Each sip feels like it satisfies me in some way, settling deep in my belly, burning my throat. I take pride in being able to hold my alcohol; my father would accept nothing less.

ALTERED BY FIRE

I start tiptoeing across the floor before I realize how stupid that is. These men are badass, and they sure as hell aren't going to be fooled by me keeping my heels off the floor. With a roll of eyes, I start walking normally, letting myself into the church with its vaulted ceilings, beams, and stained-glass windows.

It's all beautiful, meant to intimidate the masses, show them the true power of the church.

And I wanted to be a nun, I think as I move over to one of the pews in the front and sit down, taking another swig of vodka and staring up at a statue of the Virgin Mary. It made sense in the moment, when I was dripping wet from the ice-cold rain, nowhere to go, no one I could count on. After getting fucked on the altar of this church, it doesn't make any sense to me now.

Clearly, I'm not ... suited for the life of a nun. That, and I'm pretty sure I don't believe in God either. Maybe I don't believe in anything? How can I, after the life I've led? What higher power could I possibly look to after the things I've seen?

After a while, the massive room begins to blur at the edges, and I realize I've downed the entire bottle. Chucking it aside, I stand up and start to explore the huge building and all its hidden nooks and crannies. There are little rooms that look like they should house gargoyles, elaborate murals and stonework, and smaller altars along the right and left sides of the building that belong to saints.

UNDERCOVER SINNERS

There are small boxes with little slots to put money in. *Leave a Donation, Take a Candle* the sign says. There are tiny white tea lights scattered across a table and jars full of matches. I don't have any money to donate, but when I stumble upon a painting that grabs me, I stop, and light one anyway.

Saint Rita, patron saint of the impossible.

Something about the painting of her in her nun's habit calls to me. As I light candles—because one just isn't enough for the impossible—I read the little metal placard describing her life, how her husband was abusive and how she won him over with kindness and faith. Gag. Thinking about my father, about Dmitri ... well, no amount of kindness or faith would ever change the monsters inside them.

After all the candles are lit, I sway with the flames for a few moments and then debate crawling into bed with one of the guys. *You could very well be a sex addict,* I tell myself. But it's not like it matters. Really, that's the least of my issues.

I turn and head back down the aisle, stumbling slightly and catching myself on the edge of a nearby pew. *Yep, definitely time to head back upstairs. If not for sex, then at least for sleep.* As I'm moving back toward the door that leads to the living area, I spot a tall candle with a glass holder that has a picture of Saint Rita on it.

Mine.

With vodka sloshing around inside my brain, I

stumble over and pick it up, spotting another door to the right of the altar, hidden by the unique shape of the architecture in a little nook. It's locked, but I also know who has the keys.

Not Hawke, as to be expected, but Weston.

Chewing my lower lip, I make up my mind and head back into the boys' 'house', up the stairs, and into the room that Colt and West share. They're pretty adorable together to be honest, lots of bro love between the two of them.

And they feel so good when they're inside of me together, too.

Sneaking into the room, I bend down and start searching through the pockets of discarded clothes for the keys.

"What are you up to, Miss Petrova?" Weston grumbles, rolling over to crack sleepy eyes in my direction. Since I'm already on the floor, I crawl toward him on hands and knees, and then up and onto the bed.

The mattress creaks beneath me as I push his blankets aside and find his bare cock, half-erect and tantalizing in the moonlight. Tucking some brunette hair behind my ear, I lick my lower lip and stare down at Weston, nude and sleepy and disoriented. It's sexy as hell. I wrap the fingers of my left hand around his shaft, and even though I'm sore as fuck and in desperate need of a nap, I'm also in the mood to uncover a little mystery.

I'm a real proper sleuth, a member of the A-team now! A small giggle threatens to escape my throat, but I don't want West to know I'm drunk. Instead, I stare into his eyes and work his shaft with my hand, using slow, strong strokes to bring a lazy groan tumbling from his lips.

Hanging from the bedpost near his head ... are the fucking keys.

It's no chore to spend time with West, so I lean down and tease the pierced tip of his cock with my tongue, playing with the metal for just a moment before I take him deep, putting my palms on either of his hips to keep him from bucking upward. But I'm experienced enough that I can take him all the way to the base, leaning down and putting my ass up in the air. It's tempting to wake Colt, too, but then I'll never get those keys.

Weston tastes fresh, clean, a little bit like soap. He must've freshly showered. That turns me on for whatever reason, and I end up moving faster, running my palm up West's belly, my nails teasing his muscles. Just before he's about to finish, he throws his head back and closes his eyes. I pull away, reaching up and grabbing the keys in my palm to keep them from jingling. At the same time, I flick my tongue over the head of his shaft and take his cum all over my face and breasts.

"Shit, I'm sorry," he murmurs as I stuff the keys in the pockets of my sweats. Weston hands me a rag, and

ALTERED BY FIRE

I wipe up, giving him a mysterious smile and tossing the dirty fabric back at his face. "Natalia ..." he growls, but I'm already slipping out the door and heading back down the stairs.

For a second there, I just wait to see if he might follow me, but I guess the gunshot wound's got the better of him because the house stays quiet. Good. I sneak back into the church, unlock the door, and let myself into a dark little chamber with stairs leading down. Looks like it goes to the basement.

There's a light at the bottom, and the sound of voices ... and crying?

I head down the steps because, fuck, curiosity's always gotten the better of me. Even though I know I shouldn't be doing this, I keep going, creeping my way down the steps until I find myself in a huge, cavernous crawl space filled with antiques and old pews. There are old oil paintings stacked in one corner, several rickety metal desks stacked in another. All of this stuff creates a maze that I have to pick my way through in the dark as I head toward the source of light and noise.

As I'm moving, I pass by a small locked room that, based on the piles of paper inside, and the ancient computer screen I can see through the windows, was probably an administrative office of some kind. I'm not two steps past it when the door shakes and the knob rattles. A man's face looms up out of the shadows and I stumble back, almost knocking into a pile of junk and catching myself at the last second.

"Goddamn it!" Hawke snarls, storming over to stand in front of me. But I'm so still, or maybe he's just not expecting me, so he doesn't bother to turn and see me there, crouching in darkness. "Shut the fuck up, for God's sake. You've got plenty of food in there and we'll see you right when you get out."

He glares at the man in the office window and then shakes his head, running his fingers through his short, dark hair.

"Mace, I'm off to bed, okay? Just ... finish him off and we'll dump the body in the morning. If he doesn't tell us what we need to know tonight, he's clearly never going to."

"Sure thing," a deep, rumbling voice answers. It's a voice like mountains, strong and unyielding. Mace. My stomach twists to hear these two men talking about this captive man like his life doesn't mean shit. And by the look of him—the silver hair, the disheveled outfit he's wearing—he's clearly the missing priest.

"Thanks," Hawke breathes, and then he's disappearing around the corner and up the stairs. I try to remember if I re-locked the door behind me and then have a brief moment of panic when I can't decide if I did or not. For a few minutes there, I stay crouched, shaking and breathing hard, listening. But Hawke doesn't come back.

Instead, I start to hear that soft, whimpering sound again, followed by a curse. And it isn't Mace who's cursing. In fact, the person who's cursing isn't even doing so in English ... but in Russian.

Peeping my head out, I crawl forward and peer around the edge of a bookshelf to see Mace, standing above a bloodied, bruised Dmitri. Most of his teeth are missing, his fingernails. And even though I *know* for a fact that he's a piece of human trash, that he killed his own wife in cold-blood for no reason, the whole scene sickens me.

"You cocksucking piece of shit bastard son of a whore," Dmitri chokes out, but the words feel almost hollow, empty, like he already knows he's a dead man. *At least I know Mace and Hawke weren't talking about the priest,* I think as Mace circles the chair where Dmitri's bound, his wrists shackled to a metal folding chair along with his ankles.

"All we need to know is the pecking order," Mace says, picking up a pistol and checking the magazine to see if it's loaded. "And then—"

"You shoot me anyway," Dmitri says, his voice as cold as ice, like a snake slithering down my spine. I never liked him. God, there were times when he looked at me, that I just knew he'd rape me if he could, hold me down and make me scream. The only thing that stopped him from doing that was fear of another monster: my own father. "A man like me has few qualities worth mentioning. Loyalty might as well be one of them."

Mace puts the barrel of the gun to my father's

minion's head and just stands there, his handsome face stoic and frozen into a mask that lacks any hint of empathy or compassion. Not that I'd expect or want any for Dmitri, but just because I expected that out of Mace *period.*

Who the hell would've thought of him as the ... err, extractor?

My dad likes to call his minions who torture people, his *elves.* Dumb as that sounds, as soon as you see him say it with that maniacal grin on his face, lips stretched wide, balding head shining in the light, you feel that chill down your spine, too. *"They're Santa's little helpers,"* he'd joke, but it wasn't at all funny in context.

I'd seen his 'torture room' once, and I never want to see it again.

As much as I hated Dmitri, I didn't want to see this either.

"Last chance," Mace says, still holding the gun to Dmitri's head. "Tell me now, and I won't blow your kneecaps off before I kill you."

"You want me to beg? You have no idea what Konstantin would do to a rat. This is *nothing*." Mace doesn't even bother to respond to Dmitri's words, lowering the gun and blowing a hole through one of Dmitri's knees and then the other, just like that. Blood and bits spatter everywhere, and my head feels suddenly light and detached, like it's floating on the end of a string.

ALTERED BY FIRE

There are these few, awful moments where I can't hear anything but the booming sound of the gun, like the rolling of thunder. It echoes around the enclosed space, so loud that it makes me cringe. And I'm pretty sure Mace is using subsonic ammo and a suppressor, just like my father's men. Still, loud. Loud, loud, loud.

Just not as loud as the thundering of my heart, the sound of my thoughts.

I need to get out of here before it's too late, I think, but then, the booming noise fades and I can hear Dmitri making these animalistic keening sounds of pain. Mace raises the pistol again, and shoots Dmitri in the chest.

The same way my father shot Kisten.

I can't help myself.

I throw up all over the floor with a violent retching sound and then shove to my feet, knocking over some old music stands as I go, sending them clattering to the floor. I'm running from pure instinct then, taking off at a frantic pace that I know isn't fast enough, isn't good *enough*.

Mace catches up to me right after I leave the basement via the locked door and start to stumble my way down the aisle of the church. He tackles me in just the right way that I can see a flash of Saint Rita's painting before I fall to my knees with the big man on top of me.

"Talia!" he's shouting as I struggle and fight, clawing and kicking and *biting* like my life depends on it. It feels futile though, like Mace's muscles are made of steel. I'm so upset, I can't remember a lick of the training I went through today with Hawke.

Dmitri's chest exploding like a watermelon on a hot summer sidewalk.

Kisten's chest exploding.

I did that once, threw a watermelon off a picnic table and onto some cement. I was just a kid and it sounded like fun. The destruction was certainly something to behold, all those juicy, gleaming red bits everywhere. Like now. Dmitri, spattered across a basement wall ... and Kisten spattered all over me.

"Calm down, Talia," Mace is grumbling, his dark eyes desperately trying to latch onto mine. Finally, he pins my arms above my head, and I give up for a moment, closing my eyes and reliving that horrible moment over and over again. As soon as my dad screwing the enemy, it was all over. For a while there, it was a bit of fun, a streak of danger and excitement.

But not to Konstantin Petrov.

He would've made my life a living hell if I'd stayed. And fuck, the only reason he let me run away in the first place was because he thought he could catch me. He still does, too, and I know it. *Catch me, cage me, cut off my wings.* Of course, he made me sit through that awful dinner party first ...

"I don't want to be caged," I whisper to Mace, and he lets go of me suddenly, sitting back with a sigh and shaking his head. His long dark hair obscures his eyes for a moment as I sit up, my face wet with tears I hadn't known I was even shedding.

"I can't do this, Hawke," Mace mutters, and I have no idea what he's talking about. I sit there and stare at him for a moment until he finally looks over at me, our gazes clashing like lightning, sending sparks through a tumultuous sky.

"Can't do what?" I ask, but Mace simply shakes his head. "You killed Dmitri," I whisper accusingly. There was nothing else to be done with the man, I know that. He's a monster, and the second he got out of here, he'd have made it his life's mission to hunt down and kill every single one of these men. Like a trapped viper, he had to be disposed of before he shared his venom.

"You thought we'd do anything else?" Mace asks, but no. No, I should've known this was coming, shouldn't really be surprised at all, should I? As I sit there with the big man with the massive arms and the wide chest, the kind face, and the shuttered expression, I remember him holding me, naked, on the floor of the bathroom while I wept.

Mace ... is basically the opposite of Arsen.

"Why do you want me on your team?" I ask through weird, staccato tears. I'm not crying for Dmitri, obviously, or even for Kisten but rather ... for the woman I want to be that I'm not sure I'll ever have a chance to become.

"We ..." Mace starts, and I can hear a split-second of hesitation in his voice. "We had a woman with us before, and we work better that way. Too much testosterone makes a mess of things."

I raise an eyebrow, totally fucking skeptical, but then Mace stands and holds out his hand.

"Come with me," he says, his dark gaze locked on mine. "We'll get some coffee ... and I'll tell you about Portia."

My eyes look first at Mace's hand, then his face, his hand again.

I reach out to take it.

Curiosity killed the cat, right?

Nobody ever quite said what it did to the pussy though.

15

MACE

The last thing in the world I want to talk about right now is Portia. But I can tell that seeing me shoot Dmitri is really fucking with Talia's head, and for the first time in a long time, I want to take care of someone.

"Are you sure we can be up here?" she asks, standing at the edge of the tiny rooftop deck and peering over the railing. The breeze picks up the long chocolate-honey strands of her hair and teases them around her face, sticks them to her lips. She pulls them away with two fingers and glances over her shoulder at me.

"You think we'll get sniped or something?" I ask, but there's not much of a chance of that. Clearly, Konstantin Petrov and his people have no idea we're here—not the team or his daughter—or else he'd have already stormed our castle gates.

"Never put it past Daddy," she says with a sour bite to her voice. The wind is sticking her black tank top to her generous curves, highlighting a narrow waist and large breasts. She's luscious and plump as fuck, and I can't imagine why Hawke wants to turn her into the thin, lean, mean fighting machine that was Portia.

Natalia moves back over to the tiny table and sits in the chair next to mine, picking up her coffee cup in small hands and putting it to her lips as I marvel at the shape of her fingers, the length of them. I've never noticed a woman's hands like this before, not once. Not even when I thought I might be falling for Portia.

"So tell me about this mystery woman/nurse/invaluable member of the team?" she asks, running the tip of one finger around the rim of her coffee cup. She pauses suddenly and glances up, like she's just thought of something. "You must have a name for your team, right? Like some sort of moniker?"

"Hawk Security, Personal Protection, and Asset Management," I say with a slight smile, "but no 'E' on the end of Hawk this time."

"HSPPAM," Natalia sounds out and then crinkles her tiny triangle of a nose. I've also never fucking seen a woman's nose as cute before. There must be something seriously goddamn wrong with me. "H-spam is not a good team name. How about something cool like Alpha Team?"

"How about Hawke Security, but with an 'E'," I add, because that's pretty much how we refer to ourselves. My tongue runs across my lower lip on accident, and I lean back in the chair, my cock hardening and lengthening inside my black cargo pants. Can't help it. When I look at Natalia, everything inside of me just seems to spring to life. And when I say everything, I mean *everything*.

"Hawke Security," she says, tucking some hair behind her ear and taking another sip of coffee. "I can work with that. So. Tell me about this Portia chick. Who was she?"

"She was an ex-marine who also worked as a psych nurse. She's the one who ... well, let Arsen out of his cage so to speak. She literally freed him from a mental institution and they went on the run together."

Natalia looks up at me with this wild expression of confusion, like she's never heard anything so bizarre in her damn life. And this, coming from the daughter of a Russian mob boss. Yep. She's clearly fallen for Arsen's charms, too. I can tell that without even asking, and it makes me curl my lip. I know what women see when they look at the handsome, tattooed son of a bitch. But does she know how goddamn dangerous he is?

Does she know how goddamn dangerous *I* am?

"Okay," Natalia hazards, turning to face me, her knee bumping mine and making me shiver. Hawke commanded me to fuck her, but I want it to be more than that. I want her to want me, to put some trust in me even though I don't deserve it. Because the things I like to do in bed require a whole hell of a lot of trust.

"The two of them started running con jobs until they picked the wrong mark—a man that Hawke had already been hired to deal with. He caught them both, but just *barely*. And then offered them jobs. I was already working for him at the time, but Colt and Weston came along later."

"So why does everyone talk about Portia like she was some sort of goddess?" Natalia asks, her voice husky and inviting. I want to sink into it and swim, let myself drown and then drag her under right along with me.

"She was our ..." Words fail me. I'm not big on words. I'm not a man who likes to talk much at all, really. "She was ours."

That's about all I want to say on the matter. Portia lived and worked with five straight men who didn't get out much, and she had a healthy appetite for sex. Maybe not *as* healthy as Natalia's, but strong, vibrant ... creative. She wanted to please us, and we all wanted to fuck her. Hawke and Arsen ... there was something more there between them and Portia, something I never quite got to experience.

I wonder if I might be experiencing it now.

"You want me to join your team ... and be yours, too?" she asks me after a long, quiet moment, looking up at me from under a thick fall of dark lashes. "Is that what this is? You're making me Portia's replacement?"

"Hawke says you want to kill yourself," I tell her blatantly, because what the fuck is that all about? She can't kill herself, not when I've just decided I like her. Mace ... doesn't like people easily. I can be mild-mannered, I can take care of shit, but I'd rather kill most people than smile at them.

It's easier to put a gun to someone's head and pull the trigger than it is to deal with all the bullshit that comes with human emotion.

"I don't want my father to get ahold of me." Natalia looks up, her amber-brown eyes meeting mine with this pleading, desperate sort of look. "If he does, I don't even know if I'll get the pleasure of dying. I'll be a bird in a gilded cage, a doll in a fancy little house. He'll play with me, he'll let his men play with me ..." Her voice trails off, and she shakes her head, putting her fingers to her temples. "So if it's between death and Daddy, I choose death."

"What if it was between death and joining us?" I ask, tapping my fingers on the tabletop. The wind twists around the church spires, teasing my skin with icy gusts. Natalia shivers, but I don't budge. I just sit there and stare at her. "If you're going to give your life up anyway, why not give this a try?"

"I am giving it a try," she defends, giving me this saucy little look that makes the beast inside my chest growl. He wants her. He wants her so goddamn badly, like a male that's found his mate. And he'll do *anything* to have her. "I shot my father's own men and saved Weston, trained with Hawke, fucked everybody here except …"

There's a long pause where she just stares up at me.

"Everybody but me," I growl out, squeezing my hands into fists and trying to hold back a sudden rush of need and want. There are so many things I want from this girl, but it's not fair to put them all on her, not all at once. My desires are just … not as fucked as Arsen or as domineering as Hawke, but I definitely have unique tastes.

"You want to rectify that." It's not a question, but Natalia picks up her coffee and then finishes it off as she waits for me to respond. "I think I might be a sex addict. Also, possibly, a coke addict."

"We're all addicted to something," I say as she pushes her cup away and gives my half-empty one a glance.

"What are you addicted to, Macey?" she asks me as I look her over and let everything I'm feeling reflect in my eyes.

Hunger. Lust. Need.

"Justice—at any cost. I'm so addicted to justice that sometimes, I do things that are unjust to get it. Doesn't make sense, I guess, but it's the need I always slake."

"Hmm," Natalia says, walking backward toward the exit. "But there *are* other needs to slake, no?"

ALTERED BY FIRE

She turns and heads toward the door.

I wait for a moment and make a decision.

If she goes into my bedroom, I'll go for her.

If she doesn't, I'll let her go and I'll never touch her again.

Because I'm almost afraid to see what'll happen if I do.

Two sides of me war as I head back inside and down a small flight of stairs, around the corner and into the main hallway. I make my way to the second door on the left and push it open with my palm.

The room I'm using used to be set aside for storage. There's a large bed crammed into one corner, but also heaps of old shit from the church. It's a fucking junk room with a massive wooden cross leaning against the wall, casting a shadow over everything.

And then there's Natalia, sitting on the smooth blankets of my perfectly made bed, staring up at me.

She's almost looking at me like she thinks I'm going to be tame.

Makes me feel bad. Makes me wish I were tame. But maybe, just maybe, this girl could tame my heart in a way Portia never did?

"Stand up," I say, my heart pounding. Natalia gives me a look, but she does what I ask anyway. In fact, she looks almost eager to be doing it, like she enjoys pleasing others, submitting. Maybe she likes being told what to do in the bedroom? I've long since learned there's not a lot of correlation between what someone's like in the real world and what they're like during sex.

Natalia could be the strongest woman on the planet and still like being told what to do in the dark. I want to be a nice guy, but sometimes the need goes beyond my want for justice.

"Stand up?" she asks, still somewhat playfully.

But this isn't going to be playful. This is going to be quick and fast and dark. Maybe then, I can take her back to bed, lay her down, and make love to her. For now, no. No, that's not happening.

"Take your clothes off," I breathe, unbuckling my belt, nice and slow.

Natalia matches my pace, taking off her top and tossing it aside, baring her breasts in the scattered stripes of moonlight that fill my bedroom. Of course she's not wearing a bra. The suddenness with which she's exposed turns my cock to fucking diamond, so hard that if you added water, I could cut granite.

Calm yourself down, Mace, I whisper in my own mind, but Natalia is already dropping her sweats and flashing me her bare cunt and those gorgeous swells of her creamy hips. She's round and soft in all the right places; I want my hands on every inch of her.

There's a bit of coiled rope on the floor near the

junk pile, none of that soft, silky shit that Hawke collects for his needs. No, this is rough, old rope and I'm not prepared for any of this. I just grab the coil and toss it over my shoulder before I finish opening my pants up.

My cock springs free, thick and velvety, with a bead of pre-ejac glistening at the tip.

"Come here."

"You like to give orders?" she asks, but I ignore her, watching as she sways toward me in the shadows, hips moving seductively. Her eyes glitter as she stares down at my shaft. I'm not trying to have an ego here or anything, but my dick is larger than any other man's in Hawke Security.

"Sometimes," I say, because while I have no desire to be the leader of this little group, I *do* want to give the orders occasionally. Reaching up, I cup the side of Natalia's face with one, large hand. "Trust me a little?" I ask, and she nods. Not because she *really* trusts me, but because she's given up on life and doesn't care.

I want to change that.

I want to see this woman, so full of fire and passion, *fight* for her own life. Maybe if I give her a reason to trust me, she'll at least have that.

Grabbing Talia by the hair, I keep a firm grip and push her into the heavy wooden cross, slamming her back against the wood. She groans, but she doesn't fight me as I release her and start to tie her wrists to the wooden arms, one on each side, fully outstretched.

It's so sacrilegious that I know I'm going to hell.

And I don't care.

Using the long length of rope, I get Natalia bound to the cross and then tug, lifting her up by both arms so that her feet are just barely off the ground, putting her at the perfect height to fuck.

I step in close and push her knees apart, putting my cock at her opening and then thrusting deep into the molten liquid of her core. I'm only halfway in before Natalia screams, straining against her rope bounds and forcing me to slow.

"Relax," I whisper, the thick length of my shaft throbbing. I feel like I'm about to blow my load right now, this girl's so damn tight. Leaning in, I press my lips to her neck and breathe her in. Her skin smells so fucking good, like soap and flowers; I can't get enough.

When Natalia takes a breath and unclenches her muscles, I shove in the rest of the way, curling my fingers under her thighs and pumping my shaft in deep enough to hit the end of her. She's just barely long enough to take my whole length, so tight that she almost can't handle my girth.

I move slow at first, my muscles trembling and sweat pouring down my body. If I move any faster, this'll all be over, and I don't want it to be over. She looks like a goddamn saint up there on that cross, a goddess I want to worship.

No, I was never meant to play the part of a priest.

ALTERED BY FIRE

This, though, this could be my religion.

Natalia's head leans back against the cross, her closed lids cracking open to stare at me as I drive into her over and over and over again.

"Faster, harder," she says, and my self-control shatters. Her muscles squeeze around me, trying to lock me down as I pump with fast and furious strokes, taking her so deep that she cries out and then screams, orgasming and showering my cock and balls with her juices.

Taking my right hand, I curl my fingers around her hair and jerk her head to one side, biting down on her shoulder as I finish with a few, last hard thrusts. The door to my bedroom swings open as I'm coming, crashing into the wall with the sound of crumbling plaster.

When I glance over my shoulder, I find Hawke *and* Arsen standing there.

Our fearless leader has his gun in his hands, his breathing labored, sweat dripping down the aquiline length of his nose. Arsen just leans against the wall like he doesn't give a shit and yet, they're both here. Go figure.

"We're just finishing up," I say, pausing and wondering if I should kiss Natalia.

But no.

Not just yet.

Instead our eyes meet, and I can tell she knows this is just the beginning of all the things I want to do to her.

I slide out of her and step back, fixing my pants and staring at the length of her pale, white body bathed in stripes of moonlight, naked and hanging from a cross.

"My turn next," Arsen purrs, stepping close, but I reach out and grab him around the throat, slamming him into the wall. He doesn't look scared, no, more like he wants to kill me later, but I just lock eyes with him and let him know how damn serious I am right now.

"When Natalia is with me, she's mine. Don't you dare fucking touch her." I shove Arsen out the door, and then exchange a look with Hawke. "This time, it wasn't an order," I whisper as he curls his lip at me, locks the safety on his gun, and then storms out of the room.

I close and lock the door behind him before moving back to Natalia. She looks like she's half-asleep in those rope bonds of hers, so I untie her, carry her over to the bed and then curl around her, like a beast watching over its mate.

God forbid a man tries to take her from me tonight.

After I'm done, there won't be much of him left.

16
WESTON

There's so much more to this job than I'd originally thought. Yeah, I always knew taking down Konstantin Petrov was going to be rough and yes, I *always* knew we would take him down. How could we not, after he crashed one of our gigs with his crew, shot and killed Portia.

That's a sin no man could ever live down, not with Arsen and Hawke on their asses. When that man finally dies, it's going to be bloody as hell.

Playing with one of the piercings in my lip, I look up at Hawke as Arsen slides a plate of French toast in front of me. I think he likes to cook and act domestic because one day, he'll add some arsenic in it and kill us all and we won't even see it coming. He's *that* flipping crazy that he'd sit back and plan something that slow and awful.

But whatever. My GSW is fucking killing me, I'm hungry, and I'm about to get my ass chewed out for letting Natalia take those keys.

"You're too relaxed," Hawke tells me, his hands on his hips as he glares down at me like I'm a naughty schoolboy. I want to tell him to grow the fuck up, but Colt gives me this *don't you dare look.* I flip him off and Hawke slams his palm down on the table. "Stop with the high school bullshit," he snaps, "and listen to me. You allowed Natalia to take those keys."

"She was sucking me off," I drawl, taking a sip of my coffee. Colt raises his eyebrows and shakes his head. He's ten times more volatile and cheeky than I am, but yet, he's also a few years younger and still follows every order to a goddamn T. Yes, Colt and I are similar, but I'm more relaxed. I like to take things slower, see how they go. "And it's not like anything happened, so let's let it go and move on. Mass is in like, ten minutes." I check my watch and then sigh, draped in those stupid effing black robes and a goddamn wig to cover my green hair. "If Konstantin really is planning on showing up here with his minions, shouldn't we stay focused on that?" I pause, because there's this thing with Natalia weighing on my mind. Hawke isn't going to like me bringing it up, but there it is. "And if he is showing up, then this whole 'make Natalia fall for us' bullshit doesn't matter, right? I mean, what's the point of all that if we think the big baddie might fall right into our laps?"

"Let's just bring her on the team and she can be like Portia," Colt starts which is the dumbest fucking thing in the world to say. I give him a look across the table that clearly says *shut the fuck up,* but it's too late.

"She will *never* be like Portia," Hawke snaps, running his hand over his hair. Arsen stiffens, but just keeps cooking. I prefer it that way anyway, when he doesn't say anything. The bastard's too scary when he talks. "Natalia is a fucking tool to be used and discarded."

"You don't actually want her on the team?" I ask, so confused. Hawke is clearly attracted to this girl—we all are—so why not bring her on? There's nowhere else for her to go, especially after all this. Her family will be dead, the feds will be interested in finding her, and she'll be easy pickings for any of the mob's rivals.

And yet, Hawke doesn't *seem* to give two shits when I know for a fact that he does.

"No," he snaps, nostrils flaring as he stands up straight and stares down at me like *I'm* the problem here, like I'm the person experiencing extreme denial. "The last thing we need is some spoiled ass princess riding our coattails. Portia came to us with skills and knowledge, with training and practice. This girl, she's a suicidal nightmare just waiting to happen. And yeah, maybe I let myself get caught up in her. Making her fall in love with us was supposed to make gathering information easy and yet, we've got nothing. She hasn't told us a damn thing. *If* Konstantin does show up here—and that's a big *if*—then we're lucky as hell because we don't have any other leads."

"I'd just as soon see her dead as on the team anyway," Arsen says mildly, tossing another plate down on the table. Mace curls his lip up and looks about two seconds from punching the other man out. Colt just stares across the table at me, like I have some say in the matter, like I could actually get Natalia to be part of Hawke Security with the rest of us.

"As soon as we're done here, we'll dump Natalia in some backwoods Midwestern town and leave. Maybe she can find a place for herself there?" Hawke says, picking up a mug of coffee and then pausing at the sound of loud footsteps approaching the kitchen.

When Natalia walks in, she seems cheerful. She's smiling and there's a bounce in her step, but it almost seems ... too much. There's a piece of paper in her hand, too, a list. When she sees me staring at it, she smiles.

"Good morning." She holds up the list. "Groceries I need, if there's any possibility of us going out to get them?"

"That could be arranged," Mace grunts as Natalia sticks the page in the pocket of some jeans he bought for her. They're a little tight, emphasizing the round curve of her ass, and the generous swell of her hips.

"I'm planning on attending mass this morning, if

that's okay?" She glances over at Hawke, and he nods sharply. "I'll sit in the back, so I won't be a bother."

"Taking a sudden interest in theology?" Colt teases, turning on his full charm. Goddamn it. He gets attached to people too easily. It's one of his strengths *and* his weaknesses. "Because I'd be happy to join you and uh, bring about some enlightenment."

"Oh no, Father," Natalia says, pouring herself a glass of orange juice and batting her eyelashes at him. "I wouldn't want to trouble you." With a wink, she takes her juice over to the door and lets herself into the church.

"Weston," Hawke snaps, and I rise to my feet. "You're in charge of the service this morning. Colt, go make sure Natalia stays in the church—and that we don't get any unexpected guests."

He storms off, heading out the back door to do God only knows what.

"Let's go," I tell my best friend, leading him into the church and catching Natalia's gaze from the back row. There's something about her expression that tells me that maybe, just maybe she heard some of what Hawke said? I might be a tad lazy, and a little too laidback, but I'm not stupid.

"Don't fuck this up," I tell Colt, but he just rolls his eyes and shrugs me off, pulling away to go sit with Natalia in the back row.

Me, I get to stand at the front of the room and preach about things I don't believe in.

Fuck this.

As Colt starts to make his way to the back of the room, slow and casual and smiling, Natalia stands up … and bolts outside the church.

17

NATALIA

I'm not sure why I run, but I *do* leave the list of my father's highest-ranking men on the pew before I go.

I guess hearing that I'm a useless princess, a throwaway, it's struck too close to home—especially after last night. There's no way in hell I can outrun Colt or West or any of the guys, so instead, I zone in on an older woman climbing out of a van.

Because, please, I'm the daughter of a mob boss.

As soon as the woman steps foot onto the cement of the church parking lot, I'm slamming into her and snatching her keys at the same time. Even though I know it's fucked, I push her aside and climb into the van, locking the doors just as Colt manages to catch up to me.

"Tzarina, what the fuck are you doing?" he asks,

but I'm already starting the vehicle and pulling out of the parking lot, driving over the curb to get past the rush of cars making their way in and out of the narrow opening.

Sort of like Mace made his way in and out of your narrow opening, huh? I shake my head at how stupid I was last night. As soon as I saw Mace execute Dmitri, I should've left. And not because that man didn't deserve to die, but because I realized I'd walked out of one tumultuous, violent subculture and right into another.

And then all those things Hawke said about me in the kitchen?

Just because they were *true* didn't make them hurt less; it made them sting a thousand times worse.

I *am* useless, aren't I? I don't have any skills except snorting coke, partying, and fucking. I was never trained to be anything but a glittering pet.

As I drive, I swipe my hand down my face and wonder if I'm truly thinking straight right now ... or if I'm throwing a fit. Am I pissed that Hawke thought he could get me to 'fall in love' with him and his merry band of assholes? Fuck yes, I am.

But what he couldn't have known is that I don't think I'm even capable of loving anyone. I'm as damaged as the rest of those men back there, just as messed up. Well, maybe not as messed up as Arsen, but that's kind of a given. If they'd just given me a chance, they could've *asked* for that information. I won't actively hurt my own father with my bare hands, but I'm also on their side: I do want to see him brought down.

They could've just fucking asked me, and yet, they have some stupid, elaborate plot going, one that ends with me being driven to the middle of nowhere and dumped. And if that's not code for putting a bullet in my head, I don't know what is. There's no way they'd let me live knowing all the things that I do.

So I keep driving, even though I sort of want to go back.

I take an obscure back road that leads into the country. And for a while there, as the buildings and houses fall away to fields of green, I feel myself starting to relax. The suicidal thoughts haven't left me, the dark urges, the pounding inside my chest when I imagine laying out a few lines in the bathroom ... But at the same time, if I don't care about dying then why did I run?

"Because your feelings were hurt? Please," I snort, but deep down, I figure it's probably true. I let those guys get under my skin, and now I'm all butt hurt that they were using me. Well, fuck them. I was using them, too.

For about an hour, I just drive when no destination in mind.

It's only when I decide to turn down a quiet, gravel road and park for a moment—just to clear my head—that I see another car turn down right after me. Could be somebody heading to their farm or their forty acres ... but maybe not.

When I left, I stole one of the guys' guns from a holster on the card table on my way out. So I'm not *completely* helpless, but the thought of shooting Colt or Weston makes me really fucking sad. Or Mace. Oh God, last night with Mace ... Although maybe I would shoot Hawke or Arsen, just for good measure.

But, of course, when the door to the vehicle opens, it's not any of *my* guys that step out: it's a group of men that I well recognize from my father's meetings. He's literally sent in the big guns to drag me out of here, men as ruthless as Dmitri but without any pretense of being normal. These are the guys he only sends in when he needs a situation dealt with, but doesn't care *how* it turns out.

Meaning, I could be raped, killed, tortured. This is my father's last resort.

Before I can even start the van, one of the men—I don't know his name, any of these men's names—shoots my tires out while a second man makes his way toward me, shoes crunching the gravel beneath his feet as he goes, slow and calculating.

I have to be careful because if he gets close enough, he very well might just shoot me through the window. Or fuck, there could be another man in that car with a sniper rifle. I duck down and crawl between the seats, shoving aside fast food garbage and a half-empty bag of Pampers diapers.

ALTERED BY FIRE

"Natalia Petrova," one of the men says, tapping on the back window as I curl myself into a ball under the center seat, my stolen gun at the ready. It's in that moment that I really have to decide. I have eight rounds in this weapon, enough to hurt or maybe even kill a few of the men pouring out of that car.

I don't have enough to stay alive or stay out of their hands, if they intend to take me back to my father. But I do have enough to put the barrel of this gun between my lips and pull the trigger. Just like I said I would. I have enough ammo to die. But now that it comes down to it, do I *really* want to?

I hesitate for so long that a shot's fired through the window on the sliding door of the van, and a hand creeps in to open the lock. What I don't hesitate to do is shoot this guy just above the knuckles, shoving myself up and heading straight for the passenger door. There's another man outside this one, but I fire a shot through the glass and then another into his neck before I bother to open it, taking off across the field and wondering when I'm going to feel those first agonizing shots in my back.

But they don't shoot me, these men, the ones my father lovingly calls his cleanup crew. Yeah, he likes pet names for his monsters.

That means that while my dad doesn't mind if I do accidentally end up dead, he's at least asked them to make some attempt to bring me back. Or else, he's told them to have fun with me. That's a possibility, too.

Heart racing, I take off toward a small copse of trees, but I can hear heavy breathing and footsteps behind me. Doing my best to anticipate a tackle of some kind, I come to a sudden stop and throw myself to the ground, tripping the man behind me. He comes up quick though, turning and kicking me so hard in the face that I see stars, the gun falling from my hand to the grass.

A bit of Hawke's training sets in there for a moment, and I take a swing at the guy, hitting him in the face and drawing just a bit of blood from his nostrils. He doesn't look at all put off by the move. Instead, he comes at me again, stopping me as I scramble to pick up the weapon between us. He has his own gun own this time, but he doesn't shoot me, hitting me as hard as he can in the side of the face with it.

When he swings at me again, I grab his arm and, by the grace of God, manage to stop him from hitting me a second time. But holy crap, it's a strain to hold back someone who's rippling with muscles when I'm soft and useless. It's in that moment that I wish I could go back and train with Hawke, that I really could be a part of his group. Because while I've been a mob daughter my whole life, I never belonged. I wasn't a part of anything, just a kept creature along for the ride.

Our struggle doesn't last long because *four* other men approach, two of them grabbing me under the arms and hauling me up to my feet, tweaking my shoulders and making me cry out in pain. I bite my lip after that because the sound seems to excite the hell out of them.

The men chat with each other in Russian, but I don't bother to pay much attention to what they're saying—it would only scare the crap out of me. Instead, I look around and try to figure out some trick that'll get me out of this. Because brute strength and guns don't work, and that's exactly what these assholes suspect.

I need something else.

As the two men holding me start to move toward the woods—not a good sign—I walk with them, keeping up so that they don't drag me and cause even more pain in my shoulders. I just move willingly and keep my eye out for some distraction I might use to slip free. Outrunning these guys is next to impossible, but if I can come up with *something*, like I did back at the church, maybe I can make a getaway?

Because now that I'm standing here, I don't feel quite as suicidal as I did before.

I want to live? It's news to me, and it shocks the shit out of me, too.

Catching my foot on some rodent hole, I throw my bodyweight forward. Even though both men are strong and holding me in iron grips, it makes them stumble and distracts them enough for me to lift up both legs and kick the knee of the man on my right. I'm wearing boots that Mace bought me with steel toes and it looks like it hurts.

He loosens his grip enough on my arm that I get a second to yank it free, turning and throwing a punch at the throat of the man on my other side. He's too good for that though, and within seconds, he's got my hand in his and is squeezing my fist so hard, I let out a scream.

With a curse, the man throws me to the ground and drops down, pinning my arms above my head as I kick at him and he throws insults at me in both Russian and English.

"You spoiled little crack whore," he snarls as he tears at his belt. No surprise. Of course I knew they were going to try to rape me. I knew it from moment fucking one. But that doesn't stop me from fighting and screaming, kicking the man in the balls with one of my steel toes. In the distance, I hear the sound of several more cars pulling up, and my captor pauses to look.

There's another vehicle full of my father's men ... and a black Cadillac behind it.

He's in there, I think with a jolt of fear. *He's fucking in there.*

The man untangling his belt pauses and waits while several more of my father's minions make their way over to us.

"Finish up what you're doing and then bring her over," one of the men says, looking down at me like

I'm even less than the piece of meat his friend sees me as. Like I'm *nothing* at all.

So. He's going to let these men have their way with me and then what? If I know Konstantin though, it's because he's curious about the guys I was with in the grocery store parking lot.

Konstantin Petrov does *not* like to be kept out of the loop on anything. In his world, information trades as well as jewels, weapons, or drugs.

I'm gearing up to kick my would-be rapist in the face when all of a sudden, his head explodes in pink mist and I'm left with slack hands holding me in place, and a body tumbling over and spilling crimson streaks.

Shoving the dead guy off of me, I try not to think too hard about Kisten, and stand up. Legs shaky, I take off toward the woods because there's a good chance my father's just been set upon by some enemies of his. He has a fucking lot of them and rightfully so.

And getting captured by some of Daddy's rivals is as bad or worse than getting kidnapped by him.

As soon as I cross from the light of day into the shadows of the woods, I run full-tilt into a hard chest and bounce off of it.

It's fucking Arsen.

It's disturbing how excited I am to see him, especially when he just said he wanted me dead this morning. That he put a fucking knife to my throat and fucked me the other night. But maybe, like Portia, I can see a glimmer of hope inside the shell of crazy.

"Sorry about the head shot," a voice says from the trees. I glance up to see Mace sitting there with a rifle positioned along a branch, aiming at my father's men and picking them off one by one.

"I'm not," Arsen purrs, taking my wrist in tight fingers and giving me a look with eyes blazing. He pushes me aside, his tattooed arms bulging with the motion, making my mouth water. That's how fucked up I am, from one bad situation to another and I'm shaking like an addict on a comedown. Even a near-rape isn't enough to quell that horrible urge inside of me. Yep, I'm not *like* an addict, I *am* one.

"Where are the others?" I ask as Arsen pushes me behind a tree, hands me a weapon and then crouches down, waiting for my father to send some of his men into the woods. They're already coming, too, in a group of over a dozen.

"Going for Konstantin," Arsen growls out, a huge smile on his face as he lifts up a pistol in either hand—not a particularly recommended move, or one that generally works out well for the shooter—but when he rises to his feet and starts firing, people drop. I guess a flashy movie technique like that *would* work for the sociopath in the group, wouldn't it?

Across the field, I see the Cadillac with its tires shot out, a group of men surrounding the car. Several bullets hit the side of the vehicle as its engine turns over, and it starts to drive, moving on the metal rims over the gravel.

None of the shots penetrate the glass—it's all bulletproof—nor do they do anything but dent the sides of the vehicle.

But he has to know he's not going to make it far on just the rims.

It's a tactic to buy some time. No doubt, even more men are going to show up here ... and *quick*.

"We have to go," I say, moving out from behind the tree and putting my hand on Arsen's shoulder. His white blonde hair is stark in the shadows of the forest, his mouth a morbid little mask. He clearly takes joy in murdering people. "Within minutes, there'll be a hundred, two hundred, or even *more* men in this very spot."

"We're not going anywhere without Konstantin," Arsen says with a loose shrug of his shoulders, like he doesn't care if he dies.

Maybe none of these men do?

But I care.

Because I want to be a part of this ... this, whatever the fuck they have. Even if I'm useless, if I'm not as good as Portia, I want in.

I take Arsen's radio off his belt, and he growls at me, but he's too busy shooting people to stop me from speaking into it.

"Within seconds, this place is going to be swarming," I say, and there's a bit of a crackle before Hawke answers.

"Natalia, give the radio back to Arsen." Clearly,

that's an order, but I'm not part of this stupid team yet —not officially—so I don't take that order.

"If you guys get out of here now, I'll tell you everything I know. My father never thought of me as anything but another accessory for his life, so he didn't hide a lot. I'm not privy to all the nitty-gritty, but I can help."

"Why'd you run away?" Colt asks after a moment, and I can tell he's about to get his ass kicked by Hawke on the other end of the line.

"You guys wrote me off just like my father did," I say, feeling this heat burn deep down inside my belly. I want something different for my life, that's why I ran away the night Kisten died. Not because I wanted to be a nun, but because I needed a change. I don't want to be the helpless princess anymore: I want to be the knight. "I heard you talking."

"I still want to kill you," Arsen says, but I ignore him because I can already hear the sound of cars in the distance, tires on gravel.

"Let's get out of here. You train me, let me on your team, and in exchange ..."

"We get sex?" Arsen interrupts, and if he wasn't a crazy psycho with two guns in his hands, I'd have punched him in the nuts. But yes, sex *is* on order in this relationship. Err, agreement? Whatever it is that I'm trying to make.

Me, and five guys.

Makes sense that way. One man's never been able

to keep up.

"I'll tell you whatever you need to know. Staying here and committing murder-suicide won't bring down the Petrov Crime Syndicate, and you know it."

There's a bit of silence and a cursing from the other end of the line, and I know I've got Hawke to listen to me.

"Get in the Hummer, and we'll meet you on the access road."

Mace retrieves his equipment as Arsen keeps my father's men at bay, backing up until we've got enough distance to turn and run. As I start to spin away, I see my father climb out of the car, mob boss that he is, surrounded suddenly by a dozen vehicles. He lifts his chin and even though I'm across a field and buried in shadows, somehow I know he sees me.

My heart gets stuck in my throat and I turn away, tearing along after Mace. When he sees how far I'm lagging behind, he picks me up and *carries* me back to the car. Within seconds, we're peeling out of there and heading up a steep hill and around a corner to pick up the other three boys.

As soon as they're all in the car, everything goes silent. I smell sweat and blood and gunpowder.

"Fuck," Hawke curses, like he's lost something major here today. But he has no idea how much he's just gained. I'll make him aware of that though. I fucking swear on Saint Rita, patron saint of the impossible.

For a minute or two there, I really believe things will work out.

Until we come around a corner and find several vehicles blocking our way *and* one comes up revving hard behind us.

Mace turns the vehicle, puts us nose first into a ditch, and then we start to roll.

I don't remember a lot after that.

DARK GLITTER
The Wild Hunt Motorcycle Club Book #1

THE VIXEN'S LEAD
TATE JAMES

Flip the page for an excerpt of chapter one.

CHAPTER

1

In the background, the shadowy outline of a naked woman haunted a painting of lilies. The rich imagery held me captive. Reportedly the work was worth a few hundred thousand dollars, but I couldn't decide if it was because of the image or the person who painted it. Maybe both. Whatever the reason, the Beverly Hills gallery had it on its walls, which meant it was without a doubt expensive.

"Nine minutes and thirty-four seconds until security systems are back online. Stop gawking at the paintings and hurry the fuck up!"

How the hell had Lucy known what I was doing? Our comms were audio only. Still, Lucy had a point. I left the painting and crept down the corridor on silent feet. At the end a large, open room held several ostentatious pieces of jewelry displayed in glass cases on pedestals. They were part of a colored diamond showcase in which the wealthy allowed their prized possessions to be displayed for the common folk to drool over. It was a clear night, and the full moon streamed light through the windows. The moonlight refracted against the

jewels and created a rainbow of Christmas lights in the darkness.

Pausing at the entrance to the room, I fished my phone out of the pocket in my black jeans and ran an application labeled "You Never Know," which Lucy had designed to scan areas for hidden security features we might have missed in our mission planning. It took a minute to fully probe the room, and while waiting, I snaked a finger under the short, black wig I wore and scratched at my scalp. Using a disguise was just sensible thieving, but seriously, wigs itched something awful! Maybe next time I would try a hat. The image of myself pulling a job while wearing a top hat or a Stetson made me chuckle.

Seconds later, my screen flashed red with an alert and surprised the hell out of me. It was the first time the app had actually caught something.

"Are you seeing this?" It was a pointless question. She had a mirror image on her computer screen.

"Huh. That definitely wasn't there a week ago when I did a walk through," she muttered, and her furious tapping at her keyboard echoed over the comms. "Okay, it's a laser beam grid linked to a silent alarm that will trigger the security shutters on all external access points. I don't have time to hack into it and shut it down, so..."

I could picture her shrug and sighed. "So, don't trip the lasers, yes? Got it. Send me the map." An intricate web of red lines appeared on my phone, overlaying the camera's view of the room. If I watched the screen and not my feet, it would be possible to avoid the beams.

Conscious of the ticking clock, I carefully started stepping across the floor. All seemed to go well until I got within ten feet of my intended loot. Suddenly my nose started twitching with a sneeze. "Dammit," I hissed, then fought to hold my breath.

"What's going on in there, Kit?" Lucy asked, worry tight in her tone.

I wriggled my nose a few times to shake off the itch before replying, "You know how I often get pretty awesome hay fever in Autumn...?"

Lucy groaned like I was doing this to deliberately test her nerves, but I wasn't trying to tease her. I might actually sneeze.

"I think it's gone," I said, relaxing minutely, and raised my foot for the next step. Of course, Murphy's Law prevailed, and the second I shifted my weight, the urge to sneeze returned full force. I clamped my mouth and nose shut, but I lost my balance even as I tried to swallow my sneeze. My leg rocked into one of the laser beams.

"Shit!"

"Fucking hell, Kit! You have thirty seconds until

you are trapped. Get the hell out, now!" Lucy yelled in my earpiece.

Already screwed, I lunged the remaining distance to the display case. The current tenant was a ring with an obnoxiously large, canary yellow diamond surrounded by smaller chartreuse colored diamonds, all inset in a band with pink sapphires. The overall effect was a bit sickening, but who was I to tell the wealthy how bad their tastes were? I often wondered how many of them deliberately wasted their money on tasteless items with obscene price tags simply because they could.

Aware of the ticking clock, I whipped my arm back and smashed my gloved fist straight through the toughened glass. It shattered under the force I exerted. After snatching up the ugly bauble, I dropped a little plastic fox—my signature calling card—in its place.

"Kit, quit dicking around and get out!" Lucy screeched over the line at me. "Twenty-two seconds remaining, don't you dare get caught, or I swear to God I won't let you live this down!"

Satisfied at having grabbed my target, I raced out of the room and down the corridor, not hesitating before crashing straight through a tall picture window and plummeting thirty-odd feet onto the rooftop of the next building. I tried to break my fall by rolling as I hit. Instead, landed awkwardly on my left shoulder. It popped out of its socket. Hissing with pain, I glanced up at the gallery just in time to see the steel shutters slam closed on all the windows simultaneously.

"Kit," Lucy snapped, barely masking the tension in her voice. "Give me an update; are you clear?"

The evil little devil on my shoulder wanted me to mess with her, but my conscience prevailed. "All clear," I said, then added with a laugh. "Plenty of time to spare; not sure why you were so worried!"

"Any injuries?" A growl underscored her words.

"Nope, I'm totally fine. I mean, if you don't include my shoulder, which is for sure dislocated, then all I have are a few scratches from the glass and a tiny bit of swelling in my knuckles. I got the God-awful ring, though!" I was rather proud of completing the job we had come there for.

"That was too close this time, Kit," Lucy admonished me. "You're bloody lucky you heal so fast, but it's still going to hurt like a bitch getting that shoulder back into place. Get sorted then drop the ring to the courier, and call me if anything goes wrong. Otherwise, I'll see you when you get back. Stay out of trouble."

My best friend occasionally cursed like an Australian ever since she developed a Heath Ledger movie crush. "You know, most people would say 'good luck.' You say, 'stay out of trouble.' Should I be offended?" Teasing her was fun, even if my track record wasn't the cleanest. In my defense, I always got myself out of trouble without too much hassle. Lucy didn't dignify me with a verbal response and left the dial tone as she hung up to serve as her answer.

Tucking my earpiece into a zippered pocket of my leather jacket, I headed over to the A/C unit on the far side of the roof. Using it to leverage my shoulder back into place, I kept my cursing to a minimum. It slid back in with a sickening pop, and the relief had me wavering on my feet. After catching my breath, I brushed some glass out of my wig then swung over the fire escape and descended to the street below. Stripping off my gloves, I blended into the crowd. Even though it was autumn, it was still nowhere near cold enough to be wearing gloves unless committing a crime. I nervously checked the time on my watch. I had a very long drive ahead of me to get back to school and still needed to drop the stolen ring off with our middleman.

ALPHA WOLVES MOTORCYCLE CLUB
C.M. STUNICH

Flip the page for an excerpt of chapter one.

1

LYRIC

What a broken, beautiful man.

That's my first thought when I step onto the Alpha Wolves' compound, how *beautiful* their president is. Of course, if he knew what I was thinking I doubt he'd be pleased. Beautiful is for flowers or skirts or landscapes, not for men like Royal McBride. If I have to pick an adjective, I think *dirty* suits him a little better. Dirty. And brutal. And raw.

I won't let him get to me.

It crosses my mind that I'm not the first person to think that. Toni Gladstone, the woman who held my position not three months ago, she said that same thing out loud three days before she quit, announced it to the entire office.

But he got to her anyway—in more ways than one if her flushed face and mussy hair were any indication of what happened during their first meeting. *Deputy Mayor of Operations and Government Affairs.* Poor

Toni shed her title along with her skirt after only half a week of dealing with Royal and his Wolves.

I won't make the same mistake.

I straighten my own skirt—some bland, gray wool blend that I inherited from Toni along with her title—and make sure my hair is still in place, tucked back in an austere bun that's as unflattering as it is uncomfortable. But all of this blandness, this is my uniform against the world. It's a way to survive when nothing else seems to be going right. Blend in, disappear, assimilate.

I take a deep breath and put a smile on my face.

It's hard to keep it there with my eyes glued to Royal's wide, muscular back. I haven't even been introduced to the man, and I'm already falling apart. Sweat trickles down my spine and soaks into the cotton fabric of my white button-down while I try not to admire the curve of dark denim that cups the President's too perfect ass. *Oh my God, I'm already floundering here.*

I take a deep breath and start forward, my heels loud against the pavement. I parked right in front of the clubhouse, so I know the whole MC is aware that I'm here. Still … nobody's acknowledging me. It's a scare tactic, I'm sure, but these men have a lot to learn if they think I'll scare easy. I might be five two and as average as you'll ever see, but I'm tough.

"Mr. McBride?" I ask, approaching the cluster of men standing on the wet pavement, gray skies above and a row of gleaming motorcycles on our right.

I pause about three feet from him—it's as close as I ever want to get. Even from here I can feel the heat rolling off him in waves, his strength, his charisma. It's frighteningly magnetic. I guess it's not just his six foot four frame or his hard muscles that keep him in control here.

"Mr. McBride?" I ask again, raising my voice a notch. I can keep quiet when I need to, but a woman in politics also has to know how to speak up or she'll never be heard. A few of the guys glance my way, assessing, and then quickly flick their gazes back to their president.

I feel my lips purse. It's not like I showed up here on a surprise visit. In fact, it was Royal himself who approached the mayor's office in an attempt to iron things out between the local government and the MC. I scheduled this meeting with Royal's secretary not four days ago. The bastard knew I was coming.

Raindrops start to fall, fat and heavy, splattering against the pavement and the metal roofs on the warehouses on either side of the long drive. The wetness slides across Royal's rock hard muscles, making the colors in his tattoos seem brighter, moistening the eyes of the wolves crouching over his biceps until they look real, like they're staring right at me.

I refocus my attention to his head of dark hair, my gaze directed up, up, up. The bastard's too tall for his own good. Still, I'm pretty sure I've got myself under control. It doesn't matter how handsome this guy is or how nice his body looks in that tight leather vest.

I take a deep breath, meeting the eyes of the wolf's head patch on his back, framed on the top and bottom with another pair of patches. *Alpha Wolves* on the top and *Trinidad, CA* on the bottom. An *MC* and a *1%* patch sit on either side. Intimidating, much?

Well, it won't work on me.

"Royal McBride." I state his name with every ounce of authority I have—and it works. At the very least, it gets his attention.

"Who the fuck ..." Royal begins, turning slightly to glare at me, locking a pair of dark brown eyes on my face. His brows raise and the corner of his mouth twitches. Me, I come completely unhinged, heat flooding my body, filling up all the places I so very suddenly want this man to touch.

Oh shit.

Royal looks me up and down once, assessing, his gaze giving absolutely nothing away.

"Well, I'll be damned," he says, his voice holding the edge of an accent I can't quite place. He's trying so hard to hide it, but ... "Is this pint-size little package from the mayor's office?" Royal tilts his head and lets his lips twist into a smile. I can already feel the flirtatious waves rolling off of him, the charm being turned full tilt onto my frowning face. I don't take it personally though; Royal isn't flirting with *me*, not really. This is a man who's used to getting his way with a smile and a wink, somebody who thinks that anyone without a penis wants him.

Hell, it's probably true, but I won't let *him* see that.

"Royal McBride, my name is Lyric Rentz, and I'm the Deputy Mayor of Government Operations and Affairs for the city of Trinidad." I force my mouth into a smile and decide it's probably best to ignore the whole *pint-size* comment from the Alpha Wolves President. I extend my hand and pretend that I'm not studying that handsome face, the rugged cut of that jaw, the ruthless, wry humor that surrounds the man's impressive form.

Royal gives me another once-over, like he's not quite sure what to make of me. This time, I feel his gaze diving deeper, trying to get under my skin and understand what I'm all about, what makes me tick. I wouldn't be surprised to learn that Mr. McBride reads minds.

"Well, well, well," he says, his voice dropping a little lower as he goes in for yet another head to toe look. This time around, something in his expression shifts and I feel a little chill travel up my spine, dragging goose bumps down my arms. "Lyric … *Rentz,*" he says, my first name a verbal caress passing between his lips. My last name though … he says that like a curse. I know what he's thinking: Philip Rentz … Lyric Rentz. I have the same last name as the mayor.

Royal glances down at my fingers, searching, I think, for a ring. When he doesn't find it, he comes to some other conclusion and reaches up to take my still extended hand.

When our fingers slide together ... oh God. His hand is rough and calloused, grazing the smooth skin of my own with an almost tangible spark that makes me jerk back like I've been burned. The guys around Royal chuckle and I jump; I almost forgot they were there.

"You're the mayor's ... sister?" Royal asks casually, lifting his chin and tucking his fingers into the front pockets on his jeans.

"Daughter," I correct, hating that that's the truth, knowing what people think when I say it. *She got that job* because *her dad's the mayor.* If they only knew ... I got the job in *spite* of that. "Youngest of three."

"Shame," Royal says with another wicked little smile. "I guess you're off-limits then?"

"Off ... limits?" I ask as the boys behind him laugh again, all of their eyes on me, amusement apparent in their gazes.

"Yeah, I mean, how would the mayor feel if I took his pint-size prodigy daughter to the bedroom and tore off that bloody awful little skirt of hers?" *I knew it! British accent. It's faint, but it's there.*

Heat rushes to my cheeks, and I stand there dumbfounded for a second. I'm not stupid, okay, but I work in a *mayor's* office. Talk about prim, proper, and politically correct. This man's like a shock to the system.

"No offense, Mr. McBride, but this *bloody awful* skirt belonged to Toni Gladstone, the *previous* deputy mayor. I might have inherited her position and her suit, but I'll be damned if I inherit her mistakes." Royal stares at me for a moment, his brown eyes dark and deep and soulful, then throws back his head and laughs, like I'm the most ridiculous thing he's ever seen.

"Oh sweetheart, I promise not to do a bodge job on you. We'll take it nice and slow and easy, alright?"

"The only thing you'll be *taking,* Mr. McBride, is a few hours of my time and a look at the papers I've brought you. I think you'll find that a healthy relationship with the mayor's office and the people of Trinidad will be beneficial for all of us."

"Oh, I don't mind getting into bed with the mayor's office," Royal says, eyes twinkling, mouth twisted to the side in a wolfish smirk as he takes a step closer to me. "Only I'd rather get into bed with *you.*"

SIGN UP FOR A
TATE JAMES *or* C.M. STUNICH
NEWSLETTER

Sign up for an exclusive first look at
the hottest new releases, contests,
and exclusives from the authors.

@

www.cmstunich.com
www.tatejamesauthor.com

SIGN UP FOR A
TATE JAMES *or* C.M. STUNICH
DISCUSSION
GROUP

Want to discuss what you've just read?
Get exclusive teasers or meet special guest authors?
Join C.M.'s and Tate's online book clubs on Facebook!

@

www.facebook.com/groups/thebookishbatcave
www.facebook.com/groups/tatejames.thefoxhole

BOOKS BY
C.M. STUNICH

Romance

HARD ROCK ROOTS SERIES
Real Ugly
Get Bent
Tough Luck
Bad Day
Born Wrong
Hard Rock Roots Box Set (1-5)
Dead Serious
Doll Face
Heart Broke
Get Hitched
Screw Up

TASTING NEVER SERIES
Tasting Never
Finding Never
Keeping Never
Tasting, Finding, Keeping
Never Can Tell
Never Let Go
Never Did Say
Never Could Stop

ROCK-HARD BEAUTIFUL
Groupie
Roadie
Moxie

THE BAD NANNY TRILOGY
Bad Nanny
Good Boyfriend
Great Husband

TRIPLE M SERIES
Losing Me, Finding You
Loving Me, Trusting You
Needing Me, Wanting You
Craving Me, Desiring You

A DUET
Paint Me Beautiful
Color Me Pretty

FIVE FORGOTTEN SOULS
Beautiful Survivors
Alluring Outcasts

DEATH BY DAYBREAK MC
I Was Born Ruined
I Am Dressed in Sin

STAND-ALONE NOVELS
Baby Girl
All for 1
Blizzards and Bastards
Fuck Valentine's Day
Broken Pasts
Crushing Summer
Taboo Unchained
Taming Her Boss
Kicked
Football Dick
Stepbrother Inked
Mafia Queen(serials)

BAD BOYS MC TRILOGY
Raw and Dirty
Risky and Wild
Savage and Racy
Glacier
Alpha Wolves Motorcycle Club: The Complete Collection

HERS TO KEEP TRILOGY
Biker Rockstar Billionaire CEO Alpha
Biker Rockstar Billionaire CEO Dom
Biker Rockstar Billionaire CEO Boss

BAD BOYS OF BURBERRY PREP
Filthy Rich Boys
Bad, Bad BlueBloods
The Envy of Idols
In the Arms of the Elite

ADAMSON ALL-BOYS ACADEMY
The Secret Girl
The Ruthless Boys
The Forever Crew

BOOKS BY
C.M. STUNICH

Fantasy Novels

THE SEVEN MATES OF ZARA WOLF
Pack Ebon Red
Pack Violet Shadow
Pack Obsidian Gold
Pack Ivory Emerald
Pack Amber Ash
Pack Azure Frost
Pack Crimson Dusk

ACADEMY OF SPIRITS AND SHADOWS
Spirited
Haunted
Shadowed

TEN CATS PARANORMAL SOCIETY
Possessed

TRUST NO EVIL
See No Devils
Hear No Demons
Speak No Curses

THE SEVEN WICKED SERIES
Seven Wicked Creatures
Six Wicked Beasts
Five Wicked Monsters
Four Wicked Fiends

THE WICKED WIZARDS OF OZ
Very Bad Wizards

HOWLING HOLIDAYS
Werewolf Kisses

OTHER FANTASY NOVELS
Gray and Graves
Indigo & Iris
She Lies Twisted
Hell Inc.

DeadBorn
Chryer's Crest
Stiltz

SIRENS OF A SINFUL SEA TRILOGY
Under the Wild Waves

Co-Written
(With Tate James)

HIJINKS HAREM
Elements of Mischief
Elements of Ruin
Elements of Desire

THE WILD HUNT MOTORCYCLE CLUB
Dark Glitter
Cruel Glamour

FOXFIRE BURNING
The Nine
The Tail Game

BOOKS BY TATE JAMES

Fantasy Novels

KIT DAVENPORT NOVELS
The Vixen's Lead
The Dragon's Wing
The Tiger's Ambush
The Viper's Nest
The Crow's Murder
The Alpha's Pack

THE ROYAL TRIALS
Imposter
Seeker
Heir

Romance

STAND-ALONE
Slopes of Sin (originally featured in the Snow and Seduction Anthology)

Co-Written
(With C.M. Stunich)

HIJINKS HAREM
Elements of Mischief
Elements of Ruin
Elements of Desire

THE WILD HUNT MOTORCYCLE CLUB
Dark Glitter
Cruel Glamour

FOXFIRE BURNING
The Nine
The Tail Game

(With Jaymin Eve)

DARK LEGACY
Broken Wings
Broken Legacy

DISCOVER YOUR NEXT
FIVE STAR READ

in C.M. Stunich's (aka Violet Blaze's) collection and discover more kick-ass heroines, smoking hot heroes, and stories filled with wit, humor, and heart.

STALKING LINKS

KEEP UP WITH ALL THE FUN ... AND EARN SOME FREE BOOKS!

TATE JAMES

Join my group! - www.facebook.com/groups/tatejames.thefoxhole.

Like my page! - www.facebook.com/tatejamesfans

Be my friend? - www.facebook.com/tatejamesauthor

Instagram me! - Instagram.com/tatejamesauthor

Tweet me! - twitter.com/tatejamesauthor

Sign up for my newsletter that I may or may not ever send! - www.tatejamesauthor.com

Pin me! Or ya know ... whatever the correct term is for Pinterest: - pinterest.com/tatejamesauthor

C.M. STUNICH

JOIN THE C.M. STUNICH NEWSLETTER – Get three free books just for signing up
http://eepurl.com/DEsEf

TWEET ME ON TWITTER, BABE – Come sing the social media song with me
https://twitter.com/CMStunich

SNAPCHAT WITH ME – Get exclusive behind the scenes looks at covers, blurbs, book signings and more http://www.snapchat.com/add/cmstunich

LISTEN TO MY BOOK PLAYLISTS – Share your fave music with me and I'll give you my playlists (I'm super active on here!) https://open.spotify.com/user/12101321503

FRIEND ME ON FACEBOOK – Okay, I'm actually at the 5,000 friend limit, but if you click the "follow" button on my profile page, you'll see way more of my killer posts
https://facebook.com/cmstunich

LIKE ME ON FACEBOOK – Pretty please? I'll love you forever if you do! ;)
https://facebook.com/cmstunichauthor & https://facebook.com/violetblazeauthor

CHECK OUT THE NEW SITE – (under construction) but it looks kick-a$$ so far, right? You can order signed books here! http://www.cmstunich.com

READ VIOLET BLAZE – Read the books from my hot as hellfire pen name, Violet Blaze
http://www.violetblazebooks.com

SUBSCRIBE TO MY RSS FEED – Press that little orange button in the corner and copy that RSS feed so you can get all the latest updates http://www.cmstunich.com/blog

AMAZON, BABY – If you click the follow button here, you'll get an email each time I put out a new book. Pretty sweet, huh? http://amazon.com/author/cmstunich
http://amazon.com/author/violetblaze

PINTEREST – Lots of hot half-naked men. Oh, and half-naked men. Plus, tattooed guys holding babies (who are half-naked) http://pinterest.com/cmstunich

INSTAGRAM – Cute cat pictures. And half-naked guys. Yep, that again.
http://instagram.com/cmstunich

P.S. We heart the f*ck out of you! Thanks for reading! I love your faces.

<3 C.M. Stunich aka Violet Blaze & Tate James

ABOUT TATE JAMES

Tate James was born and raised in the Land of the Long White Cloud (New Zealand) but now lives in Australia with her husband, baby and furbaby.

She is a lover of books, red wine, cats and coffee and is not a morning person. She is a bit too sarcastic and swears too much for polite society and definitely tells too many dirty jokes.

ABOUT C.M. STUNICH

C.M. Stunich is a self-admitted bibliophile with a love for exotic teas and a whole host of characters who live full time inside the strange, swirling vortex of her thoughts. Some folks might call this crazy, but Caitlin Morgan doesn't mind – especially considering she has to write biographies in the third person. Oh, and half the host of characters in her head are searing hot bad boys with dirty mouths and skillful hands (among other things). If being crazy means hanging out with them everyday, C.M. has decided to have herself committed.

She hates tapioca pudding, loves to binge on cheesy horror movies, and is a slave to many cats. When she's not vacuuming fur off of her couch, C.M. can be found with her nose buried in a book or her eyes glued to a computer screen. She's the author of over thirty novels – romance, new adult, fantasy, and young adult included. Please, come and join her inside her crazy. There's a heck of a lot to do there.

Oh, and Caitlin loves to chat (incessantly), so feel free to e-mail her, send her a Facebook message, or put up smoke signals. She's already looking forward to it.

Printed in Great Britain
by Amazon